STORIES
FOR PEOPLE
WHO WATCH TV

Timmy Waldron

STORIES
FOR PEOPLE
WHO WATCH TV

LIBRARY OF CONGRESS CATALOGING-IN-PUBLICATION DATA
Stories for People Who Watch TV
Authored by Timmy Waldron
ISBN: 978-0-9994617-3-0
LCCN: 2018941023

To Corey and Emerson

Contents

I watched it for a little while
I like to watch things on TV.
—LOU REED, SATELLITE OF LOVE

New Suit Day

THIS WAS AT THE END of the good part, but right before everything totally went to shit. We were all doing these jobs that we kind of fell into and there was a weird feeling like our jobs were pretend and our lives, outside of work, were more real and we were kind of killing time before life really started and everything became awesome all the time. I think we felt famous. And for no other reason than we were young and hadn't been disappointed enough. Wait.

What was I doing? The girl, right, I was trying to impress the girl. But, what was her name? It was just on the tip of my tongue and then gone. It didn't matter. Her name would come back to me. Besides, it wasn't what was most important. What was most important were things like weight distribution, maneuverability, and timing (timing above all else). When I first laid eyes on that silver carriage I knew in my guts that it was a sturdy vessel. I ran my hand over the letters stenciled in the handle, *Tower Market*. No one would deny the pedigree of this shopping cart. Tower was a high-end private market. They had a butcher on staff and sold truffle oil in the tiny glass vials only found at expensive perfume boutiques or with good drug dealers. How the cart ended up here didn't matter. Not my concern, just my good fortune.

"It's all timing," I whispered to myself and thought about what it would take to get this done. There were a few issues. First, Vicksburg Street was an excessively steep hill. There'd be no way to stop mid-run. We'd have to ride the hill all the way to the bottom until the street leveled out. Any early dismounts would result in serious and irreparable injury. Secondly, there was a traffic light between us and the level part of the street that need to be negotiated. If we hit it turning yellow or red we'd most likely smashed by traffic. The devil was in the details, you know? The littlest things killed. Look before you leaped, and so on. "What was her name?" I muttered.

"Well?" JB threw his arms up, like *what the fuck*. His eyes were wide and impatient.

"Well what? Get in!" I told him.

"Come on man," he said. "I thought you were going to ride in the front. I'm taller."

"But, I'm wider," I said, and then pretended to be preoccupied. I held my thumb out in front of me with one eye closed. I acted as if I understood things like wind resistance, stress fractures, and sound judgment. All I was doing, really, was just trying not to fall over. This was just the thing that would set me apart from the other guys. Those unsuited suitors who constantly buzzed about her at the party. What was her name again?"

"I'm getting out." JB tried to get up. I put my hand on his shoulder and stuffed him back into the basket.

"Don't worry," I told him. "I'm feeling sharp, confident even."

"Super," JB said, and then we were off. My left foot was wedged between the metal bars over the rear wheel, my right foot pumped frantically as we approached the decline. The view of this city's lights opened up beneath us in the benthic streetscape.

People from the party lined the sidewalk like parade gawkers. Some hung out of the apartment's windows, drinks in hand. Cigarettes burned bright, disappeared, and then burned red again. Someone had flung open their car door and let music pour out into the night, a soundtrack to our demises or perhaps an ode to our triumph. I could feel all their attention, warming me, spurring me on. Our best friend, Jake, probably didn't appreciate it, as we were taking the spotlight away from the actual focus of the party. He was moving to Japan for a year, a big promotion. His girlfriend, Kelly, organized the get together as a going away party.

The face for the unnamed girl started to blur in my mind's eye. I think she was short with dark hair. Maybe I should have just tried talking to her. No, that was wrong! It had been done to death. A move like that wouldn't have worked. Not on a girl like that. No one expected this shopping cart ride. Once she saw me tame the hill, she'd have no choice other than to fall in love.

"How far are we going?" JB asked. We hit the steeper part of the street and gained speed.

"All the way," I yelled. My eyes dried out as the wind whipped my face. We were on a two-lane street heading for the busy intersection, and glory. I felt the event crescendo, and then threw-up in my mouth, a little bit.

"What do you mean, all the way?"

"To the flat part of the street, just past the light." I pointed over JB's head. "I've got the traffic light timed, we'll be fine."

"The light's just blinking red," JB said, he was correct, no doubt about it. This isn't the first time I've had such an oversight. My mind played tricks on me when I drank too much. I thought things, and then convinced myself that such things were true, and acted in accordance with bad information. It was a problem.

"You should have pointed that out earlier," I told him. "We'll have to rely on luck now." I had no idea what I was talking about, and for some inexplicable reason I continued to pump my leg. The hill was far more formidable than I first surmised. The frame of the cart started to shudder and the ting of metal became a constant and ever increasing clanging racket. It was a familiar sound, the sound of Sunday trips to the grocery store, sitting in the kiddy seat while mom pushed me through the store. This was just like that except me and JB were going about thirty miles-an-hour down a hilly street in San Francisco and I was thinking about death instead of ice-pops.

"You think it'll hold together?" JB asked, he was calmer than I expected, his voice rattled with the cart's constant quaking.

"She'll hold together," I answered.

We approached the house. I saw people more clearly. Their eyes fixed on us, dread, pity, and excitement glowed on each face. Everything seemed to slow down as we passed. I scanned the crowd and caught sight of a red headed girl standing on the roof of a Dodge. She was cupping her mouth with one hand and swinging her other arm over her head, a beautifully deep and loud cheer sounded from her. She could be the one this is all for, but no, this girl's hair was too long and the wrong color. Still, I could find her after and tell her this was for her, couldn't I? *It was all for you*, I'd tell her after we safely stopped. *I went halfway to hell for you. It doesn't matter that we hadn't met.* I saw you from across the room and fell in love. No, that was wrong. Where was my girl? Did she not exist? I gave a few more foot pumps for the crowd and felt like the prime attraction in a grand showcase.

"Try to stop," JB commanded. Sometimes I was in charge, other times he was. Obediently, I planted my foot. It smelled of burnt rubber. My foot began to drag behind the cart like an anchor in search of a rocky perch. I put some muscle into it, straightened my leg and felt us decelerate. Just as JB said, "I think we're slowing down," my brand new fancy shoe caught on the edge of a manhole cover and was ripped off. I looked back lazily and watched my shiny black lace-less leather fancy new shoe tumble down the street and then stop on its sole.

"Fuck," I mumbled to myself, thinking only of my new shoe. "Fuck!" I screamed realizing that I'd just lost the brake. It was only a moment before we were back up to speed. The intersection was half as close as it was two seconds ago. I couldn't keep my shoeless foot on the thin under bar. There was no way for me to use my other foot to slow us down. I tried shifting my weight in an effort to swerve the cart into a parked car on the side of the road, but it didn't work. Gravity or inertia or an uncaring god had taken control of the Tower Market shopping cart.

"JB, I lost my shoe."

"We're fucked," he said. New speeds were attained, a terminal velocity was reached. The cage of the sturdy shopping cart had lost its unflappable feel. It shook violently and felt as if it could fly apart at any moment. What the fuck was that girl's name? Jesus Christ, I couldn't remember. "Ethan, we are not slowing down. Make the cart stop, please and thank you, sir!" The closer we were the busier the intersection looked. Friday night in San Francisco, there couldn't be a worse time to fly across these streets, in shopping cart, wearing a brand new suit, with your roommate. "I wish you dead asshole, dead," JB yelled.

I'd wanted to point out, that due to our proximity, he should probably be rooting for my salvation, but everything happened so fast. I was no good in high-pressure situations. I froze-just as I was starting to do at then. Frozen, locked on the ever-approaching intersection wondering what kind of car would hit us. Would it be foreign or domestic? Gas or Electric? The front left wheel popped off and white sparks illuminated the undercarriage of the cart, I screamed, and then JB screamed. The cart careened left, fast, and hard. It spun out of control like a mad tilt-a-whirl at a rundown traveling amusement park. I crouched behind the basket and held tight. The force of the sudden turn was magnificent, we pulled a one eighty and flew down the hill backwards. Half of JB's body hung over the front of the cart as he tried to abandon cart. The scratching of metal against asphalt sent vibrations up and down my spine. I imagined we looked like a screaming sparkler being thrown through the night, brilliant and pointless.

It was the sound of a busboy dropping a full tray of utensils as he exited the kitchen. We smashed into something, a parked car I think. I couldn't hold on any longer. It didn't feel like I was flying through the air as much as it seemed like the cart was being pulled away from me. JB just disappeared, gone, disintegrated on impact, maybe. I hit something, heard the crack of glass and then landed on the sidewalk, skidding a few feet before knocking into a house. Everything stayed quiet for a moment.

"Ow," I heard JB moan, a disembodied voice in the night. "We should have worn helmets."

"It hurts," I said.

"What does?" JB asked.

"Everything," I told him as I tried to get up, but nothing happened. Jesus Christ, I've done it, I've paralyzed myself. It was only a matter of time. "JB," I called out. "I think I'm really hurt."

"Me too," he responded, but he was getting up. I still couldn't move.

"No. Seriously. Something's wrong." This was it. Permanent and irreversible damage, I always knew I'd do this to myself. I started to imagine my life without the full use of my limbs. How would I wipe? Would my stuff still work? I moved my head, the first good sign. At least I could use one of those straws to make my wheel chair work. My brand new suit, my first suit, it was ripped to hell. The knee was shredded and I could see my raw skin red with road rash, weeping blood. Both sleeves were torn at the elbows, but the tag was still intact, maybe it could be returned. It was only a few hours old.

JB CALLED ME AT WORK that afternoon and told me he just received a promotion and a substantial pay raise. He sounded focused and pleased with himself as he spoke.

"That's great," I told him. Even though I didn't think it was great. I was pissed. I hated when JB was doing better than me. I always felt that his success magnified my lack thereof. He was better looking, more put together, and I'm pretty sure Jake liked him more than me sometimes. He got under my skin with ease. I wanted to call him a dick, but knew I was wrong to feel that way. I wanted to be supportive, and a good friend. It was just such an effort.

"Meet me at that men's store at Union Square after work," he instructed. "We're getting suits"

"I don't need a suit."

"You need a suit," JB corrected me. "You've been out of college long enough, you'll have more job interviews and all your friends are going to keep marrying for the next five years, at least."

"So?"

"You need a suit."

"I don't need a suit," I told him before hanging up. I turned back to my computer and continued to chip away at the ever replenishing stack of papers on my desk. I continually told myself that this office job wasn't so bad. Repetitive and mind numbing for sure, it certainly wouldn't kill me. But, it wasn't romantic either, and that bothered me. I wasn't the Sisyphus of paper work, or the John Henry of filing, not even the Tom Joad of office coffee. Perhaps to compensate, my job title was somewhat magnificent: Chief Specialist in charge of Bills of Lading. It sounded more like a black-ops commando, then someone who shared a cubicle. I was just a paper pusher, pure and plain.

I looked over the top of my computer and saw my boss, Nancy, on the phone. She was smiling and laughing. Her fingers playfully tangled and untangled themselves in the cord. This was not a work call. She'd thrown in the towel for the day, shouldn't I do the same? I took out my lunch and unwrapped my sandwich. I took two big bites from one half and placed it on top of the wax paper wrapper, just so. I downed half of my pressed watermelon juice and placed it next to my sandwich with the cap orbiting the whole scene. The charade was starting to take shape. I turned back to the computer, opened the settings file and changed the screen saver's activation time from five minutes to five hours. I slid my chair back from my desk, as if I'd left my desk on some manic work mission. Something was still missing. I pulled a bag of potato chips from my satchel, opened them and even let a few spill out on the desk. My god, I thought to myself, this could be in the Museum of Modern Art. It looked as if someone actually worked there.

I spent the rest of the afternoon in this Irish bar on Powell Street, it was tourist trap, but it was empty and close to where JB wanted to meet. Any worry I had of getting caught skipping out on work disappeared after Audrey, a friendly business woman from Atlanta, bought me my second drink. She was staying in a hotel around the corner for the rest of the month for work. Her company just bought out a local company and she was training the San Francisco office. It was lonely business and she took her resentment out on the corporate credit card. Audrey was a bit older with sad eyes and a remarkably unspectacular engagement ring. As we talked, she touched my arm on several occasions and remarked on how funny I was. It seemed entirely possible that something could happen between us, but couldn't find the interest. I kept looking at the ring and imagined the honest and hardworking man that bought it for her. Her phone buzzed on the bar and an unremarkable picture of an attractive man appeared on the home screen. She excused herself and walked outside to talk.

I downed the rest of my beer and left out of a side door to avoid Audrey. By the time I arrived at the store JB was already in his suit. He looked awesome, and powerful, and not at all like the kid who used to wipe his runny nose on his sleeve. I felt guilty for being jealous of him. I should have been happy for him and his promotion. He held up a suit and handed it off to me. I looked at the price tag, and I didn't even see numbers. I swear all it said was: *One month's rent*. It made me break a sweat.

"I'm not buying this," I said.

"Come on man, you'll look sharp," JB replied. "Just try it on."

I did as I was told and had to admit that I enjoyed what I saw in the mirror. JB walked over to me, squared my shoulders, and picked a piece of lint from the jacket.

"These'll be our super hero costumes," he said.

"I'm not into it, it seems dishonest." I started taking off the jacket. "Like I'm trying to be something I'm not."

"That's the point Ethan," JB pulled the jacket back over my shoulder. "You're a loser, this suit makes you look the opposite of that, like you're successful or something. Maybe even worth it for women to be around." JB circled me. He tugged at the jacket in a few places and then grabbed my pants by the waste and lifted them up. "Thing is, we *want* you to seem like you're something you're not, because what you are *sucks*." It was hard to argue with him. JB straightened my posture, moved me to the left, and then backed me up a few steps. "Stay right there." He put his hand on his chin, nodded, and then raised his pointer finger. He walked up to me and moved me another step back.

"This is perfect," he said. I immediately felt better about the suit. I looked down to my sleeve and double checked the price. I must have misread it at first, because it clearly said: *Well worth the price.* JB cocked his head, nodded again, and then shoved me as hard as he could. He had moved me in front of a table display of shoes that came up to the back of my kneecaps. It was a game we had been playing since childhood. One of us would drop down on all fours behind our victim and the other would push. It was hysterical, when you were the one doing the pushing. I crashed into a group of well-dressed mannequins, and took them down like bowling pins. JB laughed calmly.

"Excuse me. Excuse me," the salesman called out as he hot footed it across the store. "Are you all right, sir?" he asked with annoyance. He leaned down just as I was just getting to my feet, trying to steady myself amongst the plastic body parts.

"Yeah, I'm fine, thanks." I wanted to knock JB over the head with the mannequin leg that I grabbed onto in the fall. "Wasn't paying attention to my footing."

"Please be careful, sir." He brushed off my shoulders once I was standing upright.

"I like this suit," JB said. "I'll take two of them." JB eyed the salesman's name tag. "Alex, one black, and the other charcoal. If you don't mind."

"Very good choices." His demeanor changed instantly from moderately hostile to elated. What power there was in spending money.

"And for you, sir?" Alex turned to me, bubbling with excitement. "You look quite handsome in that suit. It would be a shame to think you might leave our clothier without it." I looked at him, wide eyed, and hopeful.

"Yes, indeed it would," JB interrupted. "Ring us up, would you? Separately, please."

"Is that acceptable?" Alex asked me. I bit the inside of my lip and nodded. What kind of return policy did a place like this have?

"We'll need shoes, as well," JB said.

At the sales counter, I handed Alex my credit card with a shaky hand. He turned and ran the card. Beads of sweat bled from my forehead as I contemplated the odds of the purchase being approved. There was a tape dispenser sitting on the counter that caught my eye. I quickly pulled a piece of the clear tape and affixed the tag to the inside of my sleeve. Alex turned to me and smiled a bright wide smile. He handed me the credit card receipt for my signature and I wondered what the NSA data analysts in Utah thought of my purchasing habits. Would this suit raise a red flag among the dozens of late night Seven Eleven beef jerky and beer purchases? Surely an outlier of this magnitude would demand someone's attention.

When we walked out of the store I could feel the suit working. JB was right. I felt powerful, successful, and desired. We decided to stop at a few bars on the way to the party and try out our new costumes to see how they worked. JB pulled a prescription bottle out of his pocket and shock it like a rattle. I held my hand out and accepted the pill. It looked to be a Percocet. Occasionally JB was able to free a few samples from his job in pharmaceuticals, but he was a main office guy and didn't have the same accesses as sales. In hindsight it was a mistake, I already had too much alcohol in my system. By the time we got to Jake's party I was already experiencing rolling blackouts. The night soon turned into a series of jump cuts. People just appeared in front of me or I found myself in other rooms: eating in the kitchen, talking in the living room, pissing off of the fire escape, and so on. There were faces and hand gestures and noise, but no understandable words or conversations. But everything from the top of the hill down was a clear and vibrantly alert memory. The adrenaline must have jump started my brain.

SOMETHING CLICKED INTO PLACE. I wiggled my fingers a bit and felt more feeling come back. My body, although damaged and bleeding was once again moving and under my control. The people from the party ran towards us, they couldn't wait to see how badly we'd mangled ourselves. Where was my girl? I didn't see her. Would I even be able to recognize her?

"My car, of course. You hit my car, look at the window," Jake said. "Of all the cars on this damn road, how mine? How? I just bought this." His lack of concern for us was understandable, me and JB and Jake diverged down different life paths since moving out here. Once, we had looked to him as our leader. He said move west, and we followed. But since those days he had fallen in love with Kelly and he was moving towards a career and family. Me and JB remained problem drinkers and crash test dummies. Jake had no interest in such a life, his grown-up gene kicked in ahead of ours. "You guys are a couple of real assholes, you know that, right?" Jake shook his head in disappointment. "Kelly went to a lot of trouble to pull this party together."

"Great party, Kelly," JB called out.

"It's not funny," Jake said.

"My shoulder doesn't feel right," I said. I couldn't move it at all. My left arm, unlike the rest of my body somehow did not unfold.

"This might be a good time to take those medical benefits for a test drive," JB said. "Come on," Jake said as he knelt down to get his arms around my waste. "Alley oop," he said and hoisted me to my feet. He leaned me against his car and then touched the dent in the driver's side door. "Who's going to pay for this?" Jake asked. "You?" He pointed at JB. "You?" he pointed to me. "You still owe me for last month's cable."

"I need a doctor," JB screamed. "I'm hurt, I'm bleeding and I'm sobering up. Get me to a doctor now!"

"Easy," Jake said. "Get in and try not to bleed on everything."

"That's fair," JB agreed with a sigh. I collapsed into the back while JB took shotgun.

"You ok, Ethan?" Jake asked. His anger had faded a bit and he was looking over my wounds. "This looks pretty bad. You better lie down."

I watched the street lights shoot by as we made our way to the University of California hospital. I held myself tight because it felt like things were coming apart inside me. I couldn't prove it, but I was sure Jake made at least three unnecessary and sudden stops as punishment. Every time the gravity in the car shifted I discovered a new pain. I felt like this could be the end of me and why not? Better people have died more pointless deaths.

"Okay, here we are," Jake said as we pulled in front of the ER. "Bad load drop off, everybody out." Me and JB were left standing on the curb like wayward children at the doorstep of an orphanage. Pain continued to emerge and become exponentially worse. JB had to have been feeling the same as me. My legs, face, and back were all marked with raspberry patches of rawness from the skid. Our new suits turned to pricey rags in a matter of hours. Some wounds bled out more than others. The slightest touch of cloth to cut resulted in scorching pain.

"What kind of coverage do you have?" JB asked.

"Don't know, but I think it's pretty good."

Me and JB limped into the ER using one another as a crutch. I was surprised by the serenity of the place. It was not the guts and chaos that I imagined it would be on a Friday night. It was all but empty, just a middle aged Mexican man asleep in a chair, head down, and arms folded across his chest.

"Oh no, look at these two." The intake nurse sassed. "Lola, you better get out here quick and look at these boys." Her voice echoed off the antiseptic walls as she spoke into the microphone a la Burger King and paged her co-worker. "They are beat to hell. And one of them doesn't have a shoe."

"Aye De," Lola said rounding the corner. "And you boys stink!" Lola waved her hand by her nose as she slowly moved past us. Her fingernails were long-well-cared for pieces of colorful sparkly art. The women giggled and touched hands, there was no slap, they were mindful of Lola's long pink nails.

"Can we be helped?" I asked in a quiet, broken voice. Me and JB sank into the chairs across from the ladies.

"And what happened to you two?" Patty asked.

"We were in an accident," I said. "It hurts."

"Well, you're bleeding out of your head and that arm look pretty bad, "Patty observed coolly. "But that's for Doctor Lou to say. I'll call him right this second. Don't worry babies. We'll take good care you and get you fixed-up."

"Thanks," I said. My eyes grew heavy. I felt safe here. I would be taken care of. I would be told it could be fixed. I was part of the work force with a lovely medical plan and decent dental. I went slack and let my hands drop down next to me, the price tag of my suit spilled out of my sleeve. The scotch tape I used to secure it out of sight barely had lost its stick.

"You forgot to rip off your tag, guy." JB said and grabbed for it, with one good pull it was gone. He let it drop to the floor.

"Thanks," I said. I glanced down and took a last look at the price. It said HaHA haHAhahhaahahahHA ... ha.

"Why did even do that?" he asked lazily.

"Did you see that girl I was talking to?"

"Yeah, Martha."

"Thank you. Martha, that's her name."

"We used to fuck, like, all the time in college," JB explained. "We hardly ever even talked, just banged. In fact, whenever I cheated on my girlfriend, it was mostly always with her." His words made bile rocket up my esophagus. I mustered up what little energy I had left and jabbed my heel into the most damaged area of his pant leg. He screamed bloody murder, but there was no other movement or retaliation. He didn't even care to ask why.

Replay

KEITH FLIPPED THE VIEW SCREEN of the camcorder open, turned it on, and pointed it at the ground to test the light. Nothing happened. He was in such a rush to leave the house that he'd grabbed the wrong battery pack. Keith could race back home to get the charged battery pack, which he was sure he left in the garage, or he could just live with the mix-up and enjoy his daughter's game without taping it. It really wasn't much of a debate. He made better time than he had hoped, getting back to the game before the end of the first half. He spotted his ex-wife Christine and her new husband Marty in the parking lot. Normally, he would take the time to say hello and chat, but he had already missed too much. He ran to Sarah's field readying the camcorder as he approached. Once there, he hit record and started moving up and down the field. All other on-lookers faded into the background as he tracked the play, jogging up and down the sideline.

MARTY'S HAIR WENT ON END when he heard his wife say: 'He used to video tape everything.' Keith had nearly stepped on Marty's foot and was now ten yards down field; camcorder in hand, moving parallel to the attackers on the field. Marty watched as Keith just missed knocking into an eight-year-old girl, who was chasing bubbles blown by her mother. His elbow was so close to the youngster's head that her hair flipped in his breeze.

"He used to video tape everything," Christine had said. Her tone was light and flirty. She smiled when she said it, *smiled,* like she was lost in a specific thought. "He doesn't pay attention to anything else around him, when the camera's on." Marty's face contorted as she spoke. His head cocked to one side, and he squinted, concentrating on her lips in an attempt to figure out what she meant. The comment instantly gave Keith a kind of sexuality that had never been considered before. An unwelcome feeling of anger and ownership grew inside Marty.

"Thank God he didn't connect," she said. "That little girl could have gotten a black-eye."

Marty spit sliced orange, stolen from his step-daughter Sarah's post game snack bag, onto the grass. "I bet he's got some collection."

"What?" Christine asked as the crowd erupted in celebration. Marty lost track of the play, but clapped anyway. Christine, just as ignorant, cheered and jumped in place. Marty's comment went suspiciously unaddressed. "Way to go girls!" She screamed.

The idea that Keith might have hours of home movies with him and Christine fucking made Marty sick to his stomach. He looked at his wife as she jumped up and down in celebration. Even as the rage built, he couldn't help but appreciate her body. Her auburn hair, ponytailed and sticking out of her baseball hat, bounced with each hop. How playful and youthful it made her look. Her shirt came up just enough to show off the shape of her bottom. When she'd catch him staring, she'd say, '*The ol' tush-a-loo*', and then give her rear a smack. He thanked god for those form fitting yoga pants, which suddenly (at least suddenly to him) seemed to have become ubiquitous.

"Did you see that?" Keith asked as he ran up to Marty and Christine. "Sarah got the assist."

"She did?" Christine asked, "I missed it."

"That's alright," Keith said with a laugh, "I got it all on tape."

"Those things don't use tape anymore." Marty pointed to Keith's camcorder. The accusatory tone caused a brief silence between the three of them, which was slightly elongated by the referee's dramatic end of the game whistle. Sarah's team, the winning team, raised their field hockey sticks and smacked them together as if high-fiving.

"No," Keith said. "They don't use tape. Not anymore."

"Family!" Sarah jogged towards the three adults, bright and spry with all the confidence of fresh victory in her stride. She looked so much like her mother, but not a total copy, there was something original there; the nose, eyes, and chin seemed to come from elsewhere.

Not from Keith, though, maybe someplace deeper in the gene pool. Marty was thankful that none of Keith's looks seemed prevalent, but he feared that one day his personality would emerge from her like some dormant clown gene. "Did you see?" she asked.

"Got it all on tape," Keith tapped the side of his camera, and then looked to Marty. "Recorded, that is."

"We have to have a screening today!" Sarah grabbed her father and almost lifted him off the ground. She was already an inch or two taller than him and probably had one more good growth spurt left in her. She turned to her Mother for another big hug and then to Marty. They exchanged an elaborate and well-choreographed set of handshakes ending in an exploding fist pound.

"You got it kiddo," Keith answered. "Tell the girls to be at my place, no later than six."

Marty felt an ugly desire deep within. He wanted to speak-out and one up Keith, to invite the team over to his and Christine's house. He wanted to say, *"Why don't we do it at our place, you know, we've got the space for it, or the TV for it, or you know, the pool."* Something, anything that was bigger or better. But Keith had all those things and perhaps even his things were the bigger and better versions. He knew it was all tricked out with the latest toys and gadgets. Keith was always talking about them.

"Marty, Christine, you're coming too," Keith said. "In fact, I insist. You missed it live, but it will be just as good on the highlight reel."

"You guys missed my assist?" Sarah gave them a stern-high-whine, which Marty recognized as a precursor to a full blown fit.

"It just happened so fast," Christine said.

"Yeah, Champ, you've got a quick stick," Marty offered. "That's why there's instant replay." Marty gave Keith a friendly pat on the back. The team started to call for Sarah. The scrunched angry look on her face gave way to a smile.

"You guys have to come to Dad's for the replay." She was running with her back to them before either Marty or Christine could protest. "No excuses," she called out.

No excuses? Marty thought as he stepped up into the passenger seat of their Mercedes SUV. He had a million excuses. His back hurt, he had a meeting in the morning, he was feverish, small poxy, light headed, a pulled hammy, concussion, or maybe a nice sudden case of uncontrollable diarrhea.

"I don't want to go," he finally said closing the car door.

"Sarah will go ballistic if we don't."

"I know." He buckled his seat belt.

"That 'a boy." Christine leaned over and kissed Marty on the cheek. "We'll leave right after the replay."

Marty put his elbow on the door and rested his face in his hand. Christine liked to drive, which was fine for Marty, he was just as happy gawking at the roadside scenery. He sighed as the deep green Jersey foliage went by. He shifted uncomfortably in the passenger seat. Marty had that dried sweat feeling from the morning bike ride.

He was in need of a shower, or at least a change of his workout clothes. The word '*Everything*' kept replaying in his mind. That word covered a lot of ground, more than just birthday parties and Christenings. It had to mean a sex tape. How could it not? Christine loved to make them. They made dozens themselves. And, he didn't have to talk her into it either, which he dug. The whole production really seemed to turn Christine on and that turned him on. It was exciting. Now those thoughts made him think of Christine and Keith together. Somehow he had never even considered that Christine used to have sex with her ex-husband, even when faced with the existence of Sarah.

Would those tapes even still exist? Could they even be played on anything? Marty figured that the technology must be way outdated by this point. Although, Keith was a tech guy. He had all the latest equipment and *Mods*, as he called them. He had something that hooked up to his turn table and digitized all his vinyl for the computer. That shitty joke Keith told while explaining the gizmo replayed in Marty's head, "I only had to buy one copy of *Nevermind*. Not a lot of Nirvana fans can say that." The guy was such a clown. Was it even really a joke? Keith always let out a laugh after finishing a thought or making a point, so Marty wasn't sure. The vibration of his phone pulled him from meandering thought.

"What are you doing?" It was Sam, Marty's long-time friend. He had the habit of sounding accusatory and suspicious when getting a hold of someone on the phone.

"Nothing," Marty answered.

"That's a lie," Sam said. "You're doing something, I know it. If you were doing nothing, you'd be here with me, in *Mom's Basement*, playing Xbox."

"We're heading over to Keith's to watch a replay of Sarah's game."

"Keith's?" Sam's voice went high. "Christine's ex?"

"That's right." Marty looked over to Christine for any sign she could hear Sam's voice from the cell phone.

"How can you stand to be in the same room with that guy?"

"It's no big deal."

"Don't you just look at him and think about all the times he's had his balls all over your wife's face?"

"All right, Sam," Marty spoke plainly. "We'll have to catch up soon. Maybe golf next week?"

"Fuck golf," Sam said. "Hey, is what's her face going to be there? That hot little number from the cocktail party. Tell her I said hi and I'd still love to …"

"Talk to you later, buddy." Marty hung up the phone before Sam could finish his thought.

"So, how is Sam these days?" Christine asked.

"Same," Marty answered.

"That's too bad." She let out a deliberate breath and said, "We're here."

They were the first to arrive at the replay party. Keith welcomed them into his home and apologized for the mess, despite the fact that there clearly was none. The marble floor of the open foyer was so polished that the recessed lights from the second story ceiling reflected in the ground like runway lights. There was a grand staircase that originated across from the front door and curved left as it ascended to the second floor. It was all gaudy and femme, like set dressing from a lavish musical. Marty figured that the entire house, from roof shingles to objet d'art, was done by an interior decorator with a blank check.

"Some place you got here, Keith," Marty said.

"Thanks, Marty." Keith let out a little laugh and then waved them into the kitchen. "I know it's too much, but you know, who cares? I'm over compensating."

Marty was about to ask Keith if it was because of a small penis. He opened his mouth and just before making a sound Christine gently took his hand and gave it a squeeze and shook her head, *no*. It was as if she could read his mind.

"I know, it's true," Keith laughed. "No, you and Christine have the warm family home. I think I tried to make up for that by going crazy with the house. Besides, it was a steal. I picked it up in foreclosure."

"Keith," Christine said. "Don't tell people that, it makes you sound awful."

"It's true," Keith let out a laugh and then shrugged. "You guys want a drink or something? Pizza is on the way."

"Not right now," Marty answered.

"Wine?" Christine said.

"You got it," Keith bent down to the wine fridge that was built into the cabinet just under the island, centered in the kitchen. He pulled out a bottle of white wine and presented it to Christine with pride. "I believe this is your favorite, no?"

"Oh, Keith," Christine smiled and clapped her hands, palms only. "You *are* the best."

"You know what," Marty interrupted. "How about a martini?"

"Shaken or stirred?" Keith asked with an uncontainable smile. His trade mark chuckle, followed after it could no longer be contained.

"Your choice, friend." Marty forced a smile.

"Back in a flash." Keith snapped his fingers and knocked an open palm into a closed fist before leaving the kitchen.

The front door opened and a small troop entered the house, the field hockey all-stars, Sarah's crew. They were talking all at once, and so fast that their words ran together. It was all high pitched short-hand, indecipherable to Marty as he strained to hear them from the other room. He could only infer the nature of their conversation by way of tone, much the same way his dog, Irving, seemed to understand him. The high pitched hum and giggle loop grew louder and then went quiet. The swarm split in two groups. The larger group clomped up the stairs. The stragglers made their way towards the kitchen. Their talk became a low and conspiratorial whisper.

"Mom!" Sarah announced. She was accompanied by her closest friend, Vanessa. Sarah ran to her mother and gave a big hug and a kiss, as if she didn't expect the visit. "Marty, thanks for coming, where's Dad?" She ran around the island and gave Marty a powerful squeeze, so powerful, that a strange and embarrassing sound came out of his mouth; a hybrid of a groan and burp.

"Making drinks, honey," Keith called from the bar in the next room. "Can I get you anything?"

"Scotch," Sarah answered and got a good laugh out of everyone. "Kidding, just grabbing some food and heading upstairs. We're all starving." Sarah opened the fridge and started to pile containers of food in her arm. There was something about the spectacle that reminded Marty of his teenage years. The main difference was he'd raid the fridge after an epic bong session instead of victorious field hockey battle.

"Hi Vanessa," Christine walked over to the young girl hovering sheepishly at the kitchen's entrance. "How are your parents?"

"They're good," Vanessa said faintly. Christine hugged the girl and gave her a kiss on the cheek.

"Hi Vanessa," Marty said. He kept the island between him and the girl, no hugs, no way. "Great game," he added. Vanessa nodded, but said nothing. He still felt awkward around her, but hoped she was oblivious. Her parents on the other hand had to know. Christine and Marty had talked it over endlessly, both came to the same conclusion; there was no way that Sam's comments didn't get back to them.

Marty and Christine hosted a cocktail party—kind of an unofficial school function. They made it a point to have as many field hockey parents as possible. It was a way to get to know Sarah's friends' families. Mostly it was a way to put a face to a name, but it was also a way to size them up circuitously, to make sure Sarah was in safe company. Marty and Christine invited business associates and friends to pepper the crowd and hid any trace of an ulterior motive. Marty talked Sam into attending. He promised his newly divorced friend an abundance of single moms and hot business ladies. They hired a catering company, had a full bar, with a live piano player. Sarah and the girls were invited to have their own party out by the pool. No boys, of course. It was a flawless plan.

Everything went well that first hour and a half, beyond all hopes. Parents had nice things to say about Sarah. Guests couldn't stop commenting on how great the house looked. The food was raved about and the booze was poured with a heavy hand. Then Vanessa appeared in the kitchen, soaking wet, in a red and white striped bikini, so small it looked as though it could pop off at any moment. An ear plug had fallen out when she dove into the deep end and water had gotten in. It was something Sarah had told them about, Vanessa was prone to ear problems, and would never swim when boys were around. She was too embarrassed about the bright blue plugs she had to wear. She needed a Q-tip, and seemed a little desperate about it.

"They're in the upstairs bathroom, sweetie," Christine told the, normally shy, young lady. "You know where it is." Vanessa left sloppy wet foot prints on the floor as she hustled through the crowd of cocktailers. One of the more industrious waiters was hot on her heels with a cloth. Marty stood next to his wife talking with Sam as this exchange happened. He prayed to God that Sam would be able to break his laser trained gaze from the young girl's body before Christine noticed.

"Jesus," Sam said. Marty felt all the blood rush to his face. He swirled a plastic sword with three olives around in his martini glass. He thought about shoving the garnish holder into Sam's eye, in the hope of derailing Sam's train of thought. But he failed to act and Sam spoke, "I would eat that girl's ass."

There were enough people within earshot, odds were, someone heard. And if someone heard, they were sure to report the comment to the Davenports. Thankfully, Vanessa's parents were at their vacation home that weekend, and were not able to attend the party.

"DRINKS ARE UP!" Keith said as he entered the kitchen. He was holding a sterling silver serving tray, which was left to him by his mother. Two chilled bowl-sized martini glasses flanked a giant shaker. His friend Gary used to bartend at this great cocktail bar in Manhattan and taught him a trick where you crush up some ice and put it in the shaker so little slivers slip through the strainer and pour into the glass. "You're going to love this."

"Mom," Sarah said, peeking over the stack of food in her arms. "Why don't you come up with us and check out my room."

"Oh," Christine took a sip of wine. "Let's make sure that's all right with your father."

"Absolutely," Keith placed the tray on the counter top. "I should have offered a tour. Feel free to poke around. I could use some decorating tips."

"Go, have fun," Marty said. "Keith and I will bond."

"Indeed," Keith added.

"That's one mean sauce wagon." Marty said.

"It's been in the family for generations," Keith replied and picked up the shaker. He looked to Marty, just to make sure he was paying attention and filled the martini glass with the three-olive garnish to the brim, not a drop spilled. He moved the shaker over the other martini glass, the one with the lemon twist, and as if to seem careless, turned the shaker upside down. The liquid quickly filled the glass before smoothly trickling to a stop at the rim. *Two prefect pours*. Keith saw Marty's look of surprise and was pleased. Particularly because Marty didn't have one of his witty little taglines to vomit out and minimize the event, as he usually did.

"I should get the tape set up," Keith added after a brief silence. He let out a laugh, even though he'd been trying his best to curb that nervous tic. He had it under control these last few years, but there was something about Marty that really brought it out of him.

"Go to it, old boy." Marty raised his glass to Keith and took a sip. "Gin?"

"That's right."

"That's trouble," Marty said and took another sip. "The only advice my father ever gave me was 'Never drink gin away from home.'"

"Well, consider yourself home." Keith said and raised his glass to Marty.

"Thanks," Marty said. "Mighty tasty."

"Take a look at this," Keith said reaching for his camera bag. "The whole house is running on Bluetooth." He looked at Marty for a sign of recognition, but found none. "Wireless," he finally said. "At least, as wireless as you can get."

"Cheers," Marty raised his glass to his lips again.

Keith pulled his camcorder from its bag along with his latest purchase, a next generation computer tablet. It was a magnificent gadget, the toy de jour. His entire house could be made to dance and do tricks for him through the device. Whether he was home or not; lights, temperature, pool, lawn sprinklers, alarms, locks, garage doors, and TVs all could be manipulated from the sleek button-less computer tablet.

Keith tapped the blank screen and activated the device, he scrolled through a maze of prompts, files, and tabs until stopping at his film archive. Marty seemed to take a bit of interest, moved close behind

Keith, and looked over his shoulder. The hair on Keith's neck went on end. A warmth began to spread through his body, fuzzy and cozy. Keith tried to hold back his smile, but couldn't help himself.

"What are these dates?" Marty said. "They go back pretty far."

"That's right," Keith answered. "I've got all my home movies cataloged." Marty's empty glass was carelessly put to rest on the island. The bottle of wine Christine had left out was being poured into the martini glass and drunk before Keith could even offer Marty a refill or an appropriate glass.

"These are home movies?" Marty asked. "Those dates, they go back to when you and Christine were in college."

"Oh, yeah."

"Through your whole marriage?"

"And beyond." Keith felt Marty brush against him. It was accidental, but electric. The two men had never been this close before. Keith wished Christine and Marty had met in the old days, when they were young and wild. Keith and Christine always had similar taste in men. It was one of the first commonalities that came to light back in college, it crystallized their friendship. They were inseparable pals. He always knew he would do anything for her. When Christine showed up at his dorm, hysterical, hardly making any sense, he did his best to console her. Keith put a glass of wine into her shaky hand and sat her on the futon. When she finally came out with it, she told him she was pregnant, and he sheepishly offered to help her with the money for an abortion. She explained that the time for an abortion had passed. Christine was a champion swimmer, on a full athletic scholarship and was used to missing her period, during times of heavy training. She only went to see a doctor after her stamina broke and she found it impossible to lose weight. By that time the pregnancy was too far along and termination was not an option.

The father was some guy she met on a road trip to the University of Delaware, *probably*. For Keith, it wasn't even a question. He had always wanted a family, and he always felt that there was a good chance he'd never have a child of his own. Keith told Christine that they should get married and have the baby. If they maintained the baby was Keith's, his parents were sure to help support them while they finished college and he would have a great job working for his father after graduation. Keith was able to convince himself that it was what was best for Christine and the baby, a truly selfless act.

"ALL I HAVE TO DO IS CLICK THIS," Keith said and then pointed to his camcorder. "And it sucks the video right out of the camera, no strings attached." Marty's empty drink found its way to the island once again, the wine bottle was all but empty. "Can I make you another martini?"

"In a minute," Marty said. "I'm just really enjoying the tech demonstration."

"Well," Keith said and cleared his throat. "Once the video is uploaded to my server, all I have to do is drag and drop and it's in my video file, presto!" Keith pointed to the next room. The TV blipped on in the den and a frozen blurry image of a field hockey scuffle could be seen on the huge screen. "Ready for the replay," Keith added before picking Marty's empty glass off the counter. "Let me refresh that for you." He hopped off his stool and absentmindedly handed his iPad to Marty. "Take it for a test tinker," he said and chuckled on his way out of the kitchen.

WITH THE IPAD IN HIS HANDS, Marty did his best to retrace all Keith's clicks and flips and finger tapping, but he couldn't find his way back to the screen with all the home movie files. In part, he wasn't great with computers, but moreover he was drunk. He hadn't eaten anything all day, exercised, and then threw down all those drinks in a few quick, greedy, gulps. He was sure the booze had gone right to his head and that he wasn't thinking clearly. He was also sure Keith had slipped up and if he could figure out how to work this doohickey he'd blow the lid off this clown, *Mr. Used to Video Tape Everything*.

"Keith," Marty called out. "Gotta run out to the car, be back in two shakes."

"Righto," Keith answered.

Marty didn't wait for Keith's reply. He was already out the door. His rushed drunken strides caused him to misstep. He landed his foot awkwardly on the last step of the front porch and lost balance. Marty did his best to shift his weight mid-fall, but he had the thingamajig in hand and didn't want it broken. Marty pulled the cargo to his chest, like a football player protecting the ball during a tackle. He quickly popped up onto his feet, slightly embarrassed, and a bit dirty, but otherwise fine. Once in the car Marty pulled out his phone and called Sam.

"*Mom's Basement*, your home for electronics," the pimply sounding voice said.

"Let me talk to Sam," Marty ordered.

"Please hold." The Muzak came on, which made Marty roll his eyes. His legs were bouncing up and down and he couldn't stop fidgeting.

"Mom's Basement, Sam speaking."

"Sam, I need help hacking into Christine's ex-husband's computer to find out if he's saved video of them having sex."

"I've been waiting for this call," Sam said. "What does he have?"

"I've got his iPad," Marty whispered.

"Alright, here's what you do," Sam started talking, but his words weren't making sense. Nothing was happening on the screen. Marty was too behind the technology of the day. Normally, it was a point of pride. His first job, right out of college, was with a boutique investment firm and they gave him a secretary. He never had to work without an assistant for his whole career. Sam's voice brought him back to the device. He noticed the crack running up the side, just a hairline.

"I fell on it," he interrupted Sam. "It's cracked."

"Does the screen light up?" Sam asked with shallow breath.

"No."

"You're fucked," he said.

Marty looked out of the car to the house. He stared at each window. It was the time of day that made it impossible to see inside the house even if the shades weren't drawn. Sam kept going a mile a minute about options and servers and remote things. Marty wondered how long it would take Keith to make that cocktail, how much longer Christine could stand the high pitched tone of teenage exuberance.

"Are you listening?" Sam asked, but Marty wasn't.

KEITH HAD DECIDED IT would be a good idea to water Marty's next drink down a bit. He was acting a bit odd and felt that a little subterfuge would be best, considering the girls and all. He sat the mostly water martini on the counter and walked into the den. There was a blur of motion frozen on the TV screen. An orange mouth guard peeked through the sweep of hair covering the player's face. Keith knew it was Sarah. He looked around absentmindedly for his iPad. After not seeing it he picked up the universal remote. He pressed play and the images came into focus. The sharp crackling sound of white noise picked up by the tiny microphone on the video camera poured from the surround sound. The play went by too fast. He didn't really catch what happened. There was just a flash of movement, a whistle and then the girls cheered, and then everyone cheered. He stopped the video, hit rewind, and watched again. This time Keith caught it, Sarah moving the ball down field, never looking directly where she intended to pass, misdirecting the defense with a weak list to the left field. She made the other team feel like they were pushing her in that direction. He saw it in the replay. She took the slightest look right, got an eye on Vanessa, unnoticeable, if you didn't already know what was going to happen next. The other team fell for it. They adjusted to cover and Vanessa was left unguarded. There was a quick flick of the field hockey stick. Most of the girls on the field didn't seem to know the ball was even passed. They only reacted once they heard the whistle blow.

Keith tracked the play backwards and watched again. He felt very proud, proud of Sarah, proud of Christine, and proud of himself. It wasn't just because Sarah had turned out so great, it was because they all played their part in keeping the family together; before and after the inevitable divorce. Then, as he often did at the height of contentment, he crashed. His family, his life, and his happiness could all disappear in an instant. It was such a fragile thing, it felt real enough, but it was all built on a sham. One sentence from Christine and everything could disappear. He had begun to resent her over these last few years, because of that power. Even if she never hinted at it, he still felt her sway over him. He thought about those first years of marriage, when he and Christine were so young, just finishing college and Sarah was such a tiny, tiny baby. They lived in large rented house in Narberth, just down the road from campus, paid for by Keith's parents. They were so happy to hear he was to be married, surprised really.

Keith and Christine tried to make it work as best they could. For a while they would bring a third party home with them, always a man, because that worked best. But, the amount of drugs and alcohol they had to take to become comfortable, to get to a place where they could really enjoy themselves became a problem. On a particularly indulgent night, when Sarah was staying with her grandparents, they crushed up a bunch of ecstasy into some coke and went out to one of those loud and crowded velvet rope clubs on Delaware Avenue. Keith and Christine met a man, as they had become accustomed to doing, and invited him back to the house. Once there, they smoked some of the crack that their guest had brought with him, and opened a bottle of wine. They never made it upstairs. Instead they stripped down and went at it right on the living room floor. They turned over chairs and tables, knocked into Sarah's playpen so hard it almost collapsed. When Keith woke up, the guy (he couldn't remember his name) was going through Christine's purse. He had Keith's wallet in his mouth.

"What are you doing?" Keith, naked, propped himself on his elbows and whispered so he wouldn't wake Christine.

"I'm taking your money," the guy said softly after grabbing Keith's wallet from his mouth and putting it in his back pocket. He seemed to adjust something else back there, *a gun*, Keith thought. The guy was short and oddly built. He looked rail thin in clothes, but without his shirt was insanely muscular, veiny. His hair was odd too, cut down to his scalp, and dyed blonde, with a line shaved from back to front. He looked like a criminal, how had Keith not seen it before? Keith let an awkward, out of place, laugh percolate from his mouth. The first of many more frustrating, uncontrollable-sad-laughs to come; he was terrified. He didn't care about the money, he just wanted the guy to go, and for Christine to never know about this. He looked over to her, naked as well, unconscious in a drugged and drunk sleep.

"You should be more careful about who you let into your home," the guy said. "You got a hot little wife and a baby to think about." He nodded in the direction of the play pen as he spoke. "You can't be smoking crack and having three ways, dude." When the man left, Keith remained in the same pose, heart pounding and sweating pure fear. He was so close to losing everything, so close. Keith referred to that manic event as *the night of the two hundred and ten-dollar lesson*, but only in his head. He went out and bought his first camcorder the next day. Everything could be taken away in a moment, that's how he understood the lesson, so every moment was a cherished memory to be. Christine remained oblivious to the incident, *thank god*. When she woke the next day the only thing that got her suspicious was the lack of money in her purse. He told her that she spent it at the club. He figured she was too fucked-up to remember otherwise.

KEITH HEARD SOMEONE on the stairs, based on the slow steady steps; he guessed that Christine had enough girl time, "In here," he called out.

"Where's Marty?"

"I don't know," Keith said. "I went in to make him another drink and when I came out he was gone."

"How long ago was that?"

"You know, I lost track of time." Keith patted his pockets searching for a phone. "I think he's a bit tipsy."

"Jesus," Christine rolled her eyes.

"Hey," Keith said. "It's my fault, I make a stiff one."

"That's what all the boys say," Christine whispered and poked Keith's shoulder. He laughed politely, but really, there was no need to talk like that. There was a thud at the front door and then something smashed. Keith and Christine hurried to investigate. They found Marty standing on the porch with his hands on his head, mouth agape, looking like a guilty child, a drunken guilty child.

"Oh my god, Keith," Marty said. "I'm so sorry, I just knocked into the door and it popped right out of my hands."

"It's okay, just as long as no one was hurt."

"I'll buy you another one, I swear." Marty grabbed Keith by his shoulders. "Sorry."

"It's fine," Keith said.

"I'm embarrassed," Marty leaned in to Christine and whispered.

"You're drunk," Christine said.

"He gave me gin."

"Well, Marty, now he knows not to do that again." Christine directed Marty into the house and pushed him through the door. "I'm really sorry Keith. He used to hold his booze better."

"It's really no problem," he said picking the smashed tablet off the porch. It was really busted up. He had dropped the thing a bunch of times and somehow hadn't even scratched it, let alone reduced it to broken glass, strange. "It's just a toy," he added, speaking only to himself.

A car horn honked as a beaten down beige Subaru, being driven too fast for the neighborhood, came to a short stop. A kid in a red and blue jacket and matching cap hopped out of the car and ran to the trunk. He pulled out the six pizzas Keith had ordered an hour ago. The kid ran fast right toward the door, then realized he was trampling the lawn, redirected to the driveway, rounded the rhododendron and almost lost the pizzas as he turned onto the walkway.

"Oh, man," the kid said, sucking wind. "I'm sorry I'm late, it's just nuts out there right now."

"Lot of big games on TV today," Keith said and handed the manic kid too much money. "Keep the change." Keith walked into the house. Christine was reading Marty the riot act. He couldn't help but laugh when Marty absent mindedly reached for the martini left on the counter. Christine swatted his hand away.

"Kids, pizza's here!" Keith called up the stairs. "Replay's in five." He kicked the door shut with the heel of his foot.

Pinball Way

"YOU CAN'T TEACH THIS," Adio says to the girls that Billy kinda-sorta knew. He does a little soft shoe dance, the girls giggle. His cock-sure smile fades when he catches sight of Gwen across the bar. She's been circling him all night. Adio's doing his best not to make eye contact. They slept together a few weeks back and then never called. Gwen starts walking towards him, but she's stopped by big-thick-necked Joey, her ex-boyfriend of just a few days. She tries to brush by him, but Joey's not having it.

"We need to talk," Joey says, lazy eyed and drunk. He grabs her by the arm and pulls her through the crowd. She doesn't put up a fight. Gwen looks back to Adio. All she wants is to ask him about the promises he made and why he didn't deliver. She watches him dance for the girls. He'd danced just like that for her the night they met.

"Where'd you learn to move like that?" The blonde with the tank top and jean skirt asks Adio.

"It comes naturally," he says looking at his shuffling feet. "You can't teach this."

All the rookie cops, right out of training, wait outside for the crowds at closing time. They've spent their summer walking these little strips of sand dusted road that connect one seaside bar to another. Some towns are worse than others, but what's worse is a personal preference. Adio and Billy spend most nights here, in places that smell of Drakkar and alcohol. Places that have things called shot wheels, where all the bands play punk versions of popular, but dated songs. On Pinball Way all the arcades turn into discos after dark, and sound judgment is a scarce commodity. The crowds swell, converge, and dissipate—like amoeba life in a Petri dish. The police are already rounding up the rambunctious types. Reports of drunk and disorderly conduct pour from their radios. People drink too much here. There are problems between total strangers, reasons be damned.

"I wish we got picked for Seaside Heights patrol," Findell tells his partner Coke. Findell, tall and lean, secures a young man's hands behind his back with a plastic zip cuff. He is confident and firm, but not punishing.

"Why's that?"

"More action down there," Findell says. "They got that amusement park with all the rides and there's that place that sells the deep fried Oreo's."

"Jones says he gets laid down there every weekend," Coke replies.

"He's full of shit," Findell says. "Least I hope he is, for his sake. The only tail down there is underage B.E.N.NY tail."

"And he's got a cruiser. These bikes don't really turn heads."

"It is what it is," Findell shrugs and activates the radio fastened on his shirt. "Station, this is Findell, we need a pick up outside of Leggett's bar."

"Copy that patrol," the radio buzzes.

"You're spending tonight with us," Findell says and gives the young man a slap on the shoulder.

"I'll sue you," the young man warns. "Do you have any idea who my father is?"

"No, sir, I don't believe I have had the pleasure," Findell says. He could put this guy down, if he wanted to, he knows how to do it. They trained him well. But, he has also been trained to be polite and courteous. He is here to serve and protect the public.

"What's the story with this fellow?" Grey and stately Officer Carroll pulls up in a cruiser.

"The gentleman in custody's name is Joseph Figglia. He urinated in the 7-Eleven and knocked over a display case, caused a little damage. He then proceeded to force his way behind the counter and started eating hotdogs off the roller," Coke reports.

"It's happened before. Write a ticket, and send him home."

"Mr. Niner, the gentleman working the register, is pressing charges. Mr. Figglia pushed him over on his way to the hotdog rollers. We've got him on assault."

"How'd you catch him, he looks like every nondescript out here?" Officer Carroll asks. Coke turns the young man around. His tight muscle shirt has a giant silver 69 stenciled on the back. Coke and Findell smirk at one another. They really want to celebrate and bump fists, but they were specifically told that kind of interaction was forbidden, that it came off like gloating.

It takes Officer Carroll a good ten minutes to get through the crowd drifting across the street. The mass of club goers isn't concerned with traffic or much else. He thinks of every zombie movie he's ever seen. Finally, he flips the switch and the lights swirl on, the crowd parts instantly. Moses, thinks Officer Carroll. He looks in the back mirror and sees his prisoner slumped over with his eyes closed. Joey's shaking his head, probably replaying the night, wishing he'd done things differently.

ADIO AND BILLY STOP at a convenience store to pick up supplies for the afterhours crowd back at the house. It is well into the AM hours, but no one feels like stopping. Adio and Billy were charming tonight, and got the girls to agree to meet them back at the house. They don't have any cash left, so Adio charges everything.

Back at the house people are coming in from who knows where. Someone's already ordered delivery and passed out. The make-out games are under way, smooth voices and bubbly giggles whisper through the walls. One of the guys has become notorious for busting into rooms and taking pictures of couples in flagrante delicto with his phone. Adio and Billy are out on the porch trying to act civil, which isn't too hard when compared with their housemates.

No one is sure who actually lives in the house and who has just landed there. Some of them paid for a share in the summer house, others have just wandered in. Gwen is here. She's sitting at the kitchen table, not totally sure why she decided to wait for Adio. She tried to stay away this weekend, but couldn't sleep and had to stop by the house. Her timing couldn't have been worse. She arrived just as Adio was coming back from the beach with the girl he was talking with at the bar. They were laughing and holding hands, sand in their hair, and on their clothes. Gwen cried after they walked by.

SHE PROMISED HERSELF no one night stands this summer, and doesn't want Adio to be an exception. Plus, he seems to have everything she's looking for; he works in Manhattan, drives a great car, and dresses really well. Gwen needs to make him her boyfriend. It doesn't matter if they only date for a week or two. Even a few dates would make her feel better. They have to be real dates too, him and her out to dinner; not just fucking after the bars close. Gwen knew she couldn't count on him calling. She would have to sit and wait. Maybe this was crazy. Maybe she should just go back to Joey. But going back might just be settling. The darkness lightens and soon she is watching the sun move across the kitchen counter in the rundown beach house.

It is Sunday, and Sunday is the Lord's Day, many cry out His name on waking. The humidity is thick and with every breath they choke it down. Joey fights back the tears as his father gives him a ration of shit in front of the officers in the bike shorts. Officer Carroll keeps his head down as he exits the precinct. He has traded his uniform for a wet suit, and carries his surfboard under his arm headed for the beach. A jump into the Atlantic Ocean has near magical effects on those bodies that have been dragging. Adio emerges from the water with a little more fight left inside of him. He makes his way to the beach bar down the street. With just a little bit of light left in the day, Adio heads to the house. He packs his regrets in bags along with sandy wrinkled clothes. Still buzzed from the afternoon, he leans a little too heavy on the gas and peels out in front of the summer house. He goes back to work, back to honest living. The week is like a trip to the dry cleaners for the soul. He'll be back, next weekend; confident and ready to make it happen, once again.

Ouroboros

NATE BUTLER WAS WORKING on his front lawn the day Mr. Paterson died. The unseasonably cool August weather offered a rare opportunity for reseeding the burnt patches of lawn left by an extra hot July. Nate paused between digs to stretch his back and wipe his brow. His next door neighbor sat on a folding chair in his driveway contemplating a blank canvas and arranging his brushes in preparation of his next masterpiece. Mr. Paterson worked mostly in oils and always painted his deceased wife standing in the driveway directly across the street. The Abernathy's, who lived in the home Mr. Paterson fixated on, were not fans of the process. Besides the guaranteed presence of Mr. Paterson's wife each painting showed the Abernathy's home distorted in some perverse or outlandish way. Mr. Paterson depicted the home engulfed in flames, existing underwater, and made of marshmallows. No matter how ridiculous the split-level behind her was rendered Mrs. Paterson always stood politely, looking directly at the viewer with her hands interlocked casually at her waist. One of Nate's favorite paintings was a miniaturized and otherwise completely photorealistic version of the house siting in Mrs. Paterson's shadow. Nate observed his neighbor raise a thumb for perspective before getting down to work. After completing a painting Mr. Paterson would take off his shirt, put it on over his head *pharos style,* and turn his easel to the street for viewing. Each instillation received a fair amount of attention. The neighborhood was heavily traveled by dog walkers and families on strolls. He developed a regular following of a dozen or so neighbors who made sure their routes took them by his house for a closer look at the work.

As far as Nate and his wife were concerned, Mr. Paterson was a perfectly fine neighbor. He demanded nothing more than polite salutations, and mostly kept to himself. Well, Nate did infrequently complain about the state of their house and yard. Mr. Paterson wasn't much for upkeep and would often let his lawn grow for months at a time, ignore the fall leaves, and let the walkways remain snow covered after a winter storm. The house didn't look dilapidated, but seemed run down in some ways. It could use a new coat of paint, maybe a new roof, or some landscaping.

Nate lost track of his own work while angrily staring at his neighbor's house. How could the old man just sit there and paint while his lawn went neglected? The overgrown weeds were insane. The garage, which was left open during every painting session, was overstuffed with banker's boxes full of old newspapers and magazines. The site of the calamity agitated Nate's obsessive compulsive nature. Nate thought about walking over and offering to mow the lawn, but decided it was too pushy. He would only be asking for himself, to scratch the itch in his own brain, not to help out in a neighborly way. Mr. Paterson stood-up from his chair, arched his back, and stretched to his left, then right. He reached both arms into the air and bowed his back. Mr. Paterson started shaking his left hand. He made a fist and released over and over again it in quick succession. Just as Nate thought, *I hope the he doesn't have a heart attack,* Mr. Paterson grabbed his left bicep and fell into his easel. Nate checked the pockets of his shorts, but found no phone.

"Mackenzie," Nate called out as he ran to Mr. Paterson. "Mackenzie," he called again. "Mackenzie, help," he called one final time.

Nate turned Mr. Paterson onto his back. He was barely conscious, eyes focused on some far away thing, pupils noticeably dilating. Nate heard his pregnant wife approach from the house. She'd called 911, she explained as she hurried towards them. Her words forced as she was already winded from carrying her eight and half month pregnant frame across their lawn. Mr. Paterson looked over Nate's shoulder, locked eyes with Mackenzie, and called for his mother.

Mr. Paterson stopped responding. Nate overlapped his hands and began chest compressions. As he counted to thirty he couldn't help but notice the scarring on

Mr. Paterson's body. Each mark was medical, clean and straight incisions, flanked by little dots from suturing. Of the three he could see, the only one he could properly identify was the appendix scar. The second was high on his abdomen, maybe a gallbladder surgery, and the last was above his right nipple. At the count of thirty Nate tilted Mr. Paterson's head back, and placed his hand underneath the old man. He took a short powerful breath, blinked purposefully and told himself to focus. Nate caught site of what would become the last driveway painting lying on the ground next to them. Instead of another perversion of Abernathy's home Mr. Paterson had painted a sky-blue blob. Maybe it was a swimming pool from above? There was too much design and purpose to the shape for it just to be a careless blotch. It was both basic and fascinating. Looking at it made him feel calm and detached. Nate pulled himself back into the moment, checked Mr. Paterson's mouth and throat for obstructions and then administered mouth to mouth. He knew as soon his mouth touched Mr. Paterson's that the body was beyond revival.

"He's gone," Nate said.

"Fuck," Mackenzie said. "My water broke."

❖
❖

AT 3:48AM THE BABY CRIED, waking Nate from the light slumber of a new parent. His wife wore ear plugs on her "off" nights and did not stir. There was a bottle of breast milk on his night stand, which he grabbed before making his way to the nursery. Despite the abundance of fans and white noise machines Nate could hear the dull thump of bass coming from the house next door. He picked his four month-old son, Douglas, out of the crib. The bottle quickly mollified the tiny cries. Nate walked circles in the nursery doing his best to soothe the sleepy, yet agitated child. He turned on a turtle shaped toy with plastic blue shell and plushy bottom. A calm and tranquil light shot from its back and projected a brilliant shallow sea scape on the ceiling. Douglas entranced by the light show, settled. Nate paused by the window and looked down to what he and his wife had come to call *the party house*. After Mr. Paterson passed the house went up for auction in an estate sale. The new owner purchased the house as an investment property and rented it out. The boom of bass and roar of a substantial crowd peaked for a quick moment as a young man exited the rear of the house. He stood on the back deck, wearing work boots, tighty whities, and an orange vest. The young man stroked his bushy brown beard, then gathered his long hair with both hands and twisted it around into a man bun. Nate let out a judgy breath. The young man casually sifted through trash on the table. He shook out a few jackets left on chairs, and finally found what he was looking for. Whatever he found was lit, and smoked. He arched his back in between drags, letting his round white belly breach the cold night air. The young man carried himself in a way that seemed familiar to Nate. He had the gate of an ex-football player, someone who may have once been powerful, but had gone soft. In that way, the young man seemed relatable to Nate. The noise spiked again as the door to the deck opened. The murmur of a party patter rushed out. The young man nodded to the person at the door, put out his smoke, and returned inside. Nate rocked back and forth, counted to one hundred, and returned the sleeping child back to his crib.

Any day that Douglas slept past 6:00AM was taken as a miracle. The Butlers celebrated this reprieve from parenting by lying in bed with their phones inches from their face scrolling through screen after screen of blissfully useless unimportant information. Just before 7:00AM the short breaths of frustration became audible in the next room. Their dog, Slainte, was similarly shell-shocked by this new addition and groaned from the foot of the bed. Mackenzie mumbled *baby* as she got out of bed. Her husband followed. She thought he said *garbage* as he made his way down the stairs, but wasn't sure, and didn't really care. Douglas was wide awake in his crib, seemingly chilled-out now that Mom was in sight. She thought about letting him be for a moment, but it was impossible not to pick him up, to not hold him, to not rest her nose against the top of his head and inhale deeply. Mackenzie sang her good morning song, made up of misremembered lyrics to a tune from *Singing in the Rain* and he smiled and laughed, which made her smile and laugh. She held him to her sore swollen breast and bounced him while pacing the room. Mackenzie caught sight of Nate from the nursery window. He was walking away from the trash bin at the curb and over toward the party house. She briefly thought that last night's festivities may have been the last straw for him. The young man with a beard made his way towards her husband with his hand out. The two shook hands and began to speak. From the nursery window, the exchange seemed pleasant enough. Douglas squirmed in her arms and she said, "Ok," to him softly. "Shhh, shhh, shhh."

❖❖

NATE SPOTTED THE YOUNG bearded guy after dragging the trash bin to the curb. He stared at his new neighbor while contemplating what to do, and how to make an introduction. Should he be indignant about the late night parties? Or should he be neighborly and give the guy a chance to adjust to suburban living? In mid-debate the young bearded guy looked Nate's way and waved. Nate smiled, waved back, and walked toward his neighbor.

"How's it going?" Nate asked.

"Good, good," The young neighbor said. "Sorry I haven't been by to introduce myself, I'm still getting settled."

"No, no problem," Nate said. They shook hands. Nate could smell the booze and smoke wafting off of him. He was still shirtless under the vest, but thankfully had since put on pants.

"Well, welcome to the neighborhood…" Nate shook his head, squinted, and forced a smile.

"Nate," The young bearded guy said.

"Right, and you're?"

"Nate," the young bearded guy repeated.

"I'm Nate," the two men said simultaneously while pointing to themselves with their thumbs.

"No fucking way," Young bearded guy said, laughing and leaning back. "We've got the same name."

"Guess so." Nate grimaced. Young bearded Nate continued to laugh and held up his hand to high-five, which was awkwardly accommodated. "Listen," Nate finally said. "We have a four month-old, and we'd appreciate it if you can keep the all-night parties to a minimum."

"Oh, sure." He stopped laughing. "I'll keep it to a dull roar."

"That's not exactly what I'm asking," Nate said. He heard an urgent knocking sound and turned back to the house. His wife stood in the center of the picture window, holding the baby and waving him over to her. "I've gotta go."

◇◇
◇◇

MACKENZIE NEEDED TO PUMP, *like whoa*. Some mornings were fine and others were an avalanche of pain. It was like gravity had an extra strong hold on her insides, every time she stepped a weighty electric discomfort zapped through her. When Nate entered the house the dog went ballistic and caused the baby to cry. It was just too fucking much. And on top of all the noise her tits were about to explode.

"So the bearded guy next door..." Nate began to say.

"Take the baby," she said, almost as an afterthought, handed Douglas to Nate and made a slow but determined B-line for her breast pump. The process of putting on the contraption was second nature. The real issue, the thing that made the whole affair an ordeal, was the drain she felt while pumping. In the first month she couldn't do it without crying. The *Let-Down,* as it was called on the *Mommy Boards* was described as a warm tingling feeling in the breast while the baby nursed. As Mackenzie experienced it, the *Let-Down* was a hormone surge that arrived in the form of depression and dread. She quickly learned to keep distracted while expressing milk. Her iPad was ideal. She'd read a bit of a book, hit a few websites, and then eventually land back on the *Mommy Boards*. For the most part the *Mommy Boards* provided a mix of practical advice, voyeuristic entertainment, and eye rolling commiserating. She created a user account at the insistence of her neighbor Jenny Abernathy. Jenny swore they were a lifesaver when she had her daughter Cindy a few years earlier. Although Mackenzie hadn't ever directly interacted with others on the board she found it legitimately helpful for a time. The information which once seemed revelatory sat stale on the screen. She'd even gone through months, if not years, of archived posts. After six months they all repeated themselves. It was like an online high school where new moms graduated and a new crop came in, reading the same books, and stirring up the same drama. The darkness of the impending *Let-Down* swelled inside her. She logged-in as mothersattva365 and typed a post saying she suspected her husband of cheating on her. She hastily revised it to read that she had found videos on her husband's laptop. *Pornography*, she thought to herself, no, *bestiality!* She wrote, reread her work, and felt she'd nailed the tone. She hit send. *I found bestiality videos on my husband's laptop and the dog is acting strange. I'm not sure what to do.* The reaction was immediate and better and more distracting than she could have hoped.

❖❖

CAR DOORS STARTED TO SLAM at all hours of the night, each one set the dog off, and then the dog set off the baby. Mackenzie woke up crazy annoyed. She went through a number of different scenarios subtly differing by degrees. The politest involved some mild stalking and a casual run-in outside, like how Nate met the other Nate. The most severe involved a bag of Slainte's shit on their front door and the word *Quiet* painted in lamb's blood. Another door slammed. She shot out of bed. There was no time to wait for an opportune moment or for Slainte's next bowel movement. She heard the sounds of Nate humming a lullaby to Douglas as she crept down the hallway. A warm blue light from the toy turtle's seascape night-light spilled from the slightly ajar door. The child's toy never ceased to catch her eye. She stared at the warm Caribbean colors and rhythmic movement of light calmed her. Another car door slammed and she was back on her original mission.

Mackenzie put on her winter coat and made her way to the neighbor's house. A group of three people were leaning on a running car smoking cigarettes and chatting. They seemed to quiet as she crossed the lawn. One by one they put out their smokes and got into the car. She heard one of them say, "She mad."

Mackenzie was familiar with the modus operandi of a dealer. It was, after all, how she put herself through college. But, when she was in the game, it was out of dorms and apartments in student ghettos. Shit could be loud at all hours because there were no fucking families. She'd never set-up shop in the suburbs, even back then, she knew better. It was stupid, inconsiderate, and a bad business practice. Mackenzie stopped herself from ringing the bell and opted to bang on the door with a clenched fist. It felt more confrontational and dickish. A young woman answered the door in a bright and spry way that made her question the time of night. She panicked at the thought that it might be too early for the late night noise complaint she was ready to volley.

"Do you know what time it is?" Mackenzie asked sounding as irritated as she could.

"You came over here to ask the time?" The young woman looked over her shoulder to Other Nate, sitting on the couch, and watching TV in his underwear. "Nate, the neighbor's here."

"Invite her in," he said, without looking away from a *Friends* episode that Mackenzie remembered from its first run—*The One with the Flashback*. The young woman stood back, opened the door further and motioned for Mackenzie to enter. Mackenzie squinted at the young woman. There was something about this woman, the way she stood—her *couldn't give a shit* attitude, those boots, and that shirt (but mostly the boots). She liked this girl and she normally didn't take to other women.

"This isn't a social visit," Mackenzie said walking into the house.

"No?" the young woman asked.

"Do you live here too?"

"That's right," she said and offered her hand. "I'm renting a room from Nate, my name is Mackenzie."

"Is this some kind of joke?"

"Is what a joke?"

"Her name is Mackenzie too," Other Nate said from the couch. "She thinks you're fucking with her."

"I don't give a shit if your name is Mackenzie or Jesus Fucking Christ," Mackenzie said. "I know you're dealing and it needs to stop." Other Nate and Other Mackenzie kept looking at her, but offered no response. "This is family neighborhood," she said.

"Well," Other Mackenzie put her arm on Mackenzie's shoulder and led her to the love seat. "Sit, have a vape, let's talk this over." Other Mackenzie took an inflated clear plastic bag off of what looked to be the base of a blender and handed to Mackenzie. "We can't just stop, but maybe we can amend our hours. Say no pick-ups after eleven."

"No pick-ups after eight, and I won't call the cops." Mackenzie put the plunger of the bag in her mouth and inhaled deeply. The neutered taste of marijuana filled her mouth, and a sense of relief, long absent from her life glowed inside her. She exhaled and leaned back into the love seat. "Not bad," she said and nodded to Other Mackenzie and Other Nate. They sat there quietly for a few moments and watched television and didn't talk to one another for a bit. Mackenzie felt happier than she had in weeks.

"What's that blue light coming from your house?" Other Nate said after a bit. He was looking past the television and out the side window.

"That's our turtle," Mackenzie said. "He's a toy that shoots calming blue light out of his back."

"The light is hypnotic," Other Mackenzie said.

"It helps Douglas go to sleep," Mackenzie said.

"It reminds me of something," Other Nate said just before dozing off.

❖❖

THE MOST RECENT COLD SNAP came to an end leaving a rare balmy sixty-five degree December day in its wake. Nate was determined to take full advantage of the unseasonably warm day by walking around the neighborhood with the family. The circular and interconnected layout of their neighborhood was ideal for family walks. Nate, Mackenzie, Douglas, and Slainte could cover five miles of ground, and never be more than a mile away from home. This proved advantageous when Douglas had diaper blow-outs or got sick or any other number of surprising baby related emergencies that frequently caught them by surprise. Midway through their second lap the family hit their stride. Mackenzie pushed Douglas along while Nate assertively steered Slainte past any number of noteworthy sniffing spots. They were coming up on their house and having such a fine time that they decided to keep going.

"You shouldn't be allowed to own a dog." A call came from across the street. Nate stopped and turned, finding his neighbor, Scott Abernathy, standing on his lawn in his bathrobe.

"It's a free country, Scott," Nate replied. "And quite frankly, it's none of your business." Scott was an angry over the hill high-school administrator obsessed with maintaining certain esthetics in the neighborhood. Nate wasn't surprised that Scott rushed outside and shouted something ridiculous to him. However, he was surprised that Scott was angry enough to march toward him with, what seemed to be, the initiation of a physical confrontation. Nate puffed out his chest and wrapped Slainte's leash around his hand. Scott's wife, Jenny, was vigilant and always on alert to temper her husband's aggressive civic concerns. She rushed out the front door calling after her husband. Scott ignored

Jenny until she caught up with him and grabbed him by the arm and turned him to see his three-year-old daughter watching them through the window. The two exchanged hushed, but urgent words until Scott threw his hands up in the air and returned inside.

"What the fuck was that?" Nate asked.

"I have to catch you up on a joke," Mackenzie said. "Have I ever told you about those Mommy Boards?" Mackenzie casually told Nate about how Jenny Abernathy had directed her to numerous mommycentic blogs and message boards that had been of help to Jenny when Cindy was born. Mackenzie forgot that Jenny helped set-up most of her accounts and knew her user name. A fact that was totally forgotten when Mackenzie started to troll the other moms with news that her husband might make the dog lick peanut butter off of his balls. As their largely pedantic argument continued on without a foreseeable end, Mackenzie let slip that she spent an evening hanging out with their neighbors in the *party house*. The admission was more of a desperate attempt to move on to another topic, rather than a slipup.

"What is wrong with you," Nate finally interrupted. "We have a kid, you're a mom. You can't get high with the neighbors and post nonsense on the internet."

"Becoming a dad has made you a total pussy," Mackenzie said. They stood silently looking at one another. Nate attempted to speak, but only mustered a frustrated noise before walking out of the room.

❖❖
❖❖

DOUGLAS'S CRYING PULLED NATE from sleep. He robot-ically rose from bed, grabbed the bottle of breast milk off his nightstand, and went to his son's room. Douglas, as part of his current routine, stopped crying as the door opened. All the books and articles Nate read stressed how he shouldn't do anything to engage the baby during night feedings, but the sight of his son's smile made him happy in a way nothing else ever had. He scooped Douglas from the crib, smiled back and baby talked nonsense words, confessed his love, and made any noise that he knew would illicit a smile or giggle. Nate situated Douglas for his feeding, put the bottle in the boy's mouth and then walked to the dresser. The turtle was not in his usual spot, but it was late, and Nate was unconcerned with the absence. Douglas settled and seemed content with the bottle. Nate continued to circle the room until the boy no longer drank or squirmed in his arms. Semi-confident that Douglas was asleep Nate stopped his pacing and stood at the side window. He gently rocked the boy back and forth, watch the boy's heavy eyes. Nate looked up and noticed a familiar look-ing blue light coming from *the party house*. The thought that it might come from Douglas's turtle sent a shot of adrenaline through his body.

Feeling sure and righteous, Nate went into his room ready to wake his wife. The bed was empty. He quietly searched the house. Each empty room fed a nagging feeling that she'd gone next door. All the anger from their earlier argument became crystalline. He pulled on his snow boots, put on a hunting cap, wrapped Douglas in a blanket, and walked next door. *Shock and Awe*, he thought to himself. What are they going to say to a forty-year old man standing in his underwear holding a baby? *Nothing, that's what you say to that.*

Nate walked out of his front door and through his neighbors back gate. He saw the blue sparkling light of the turtle spill out onto the deck. He put his face up against the sliding glass door. No one flinched. He pulled the door open expecting to be hit with noise and pot smoke, but it was quiet with just a hint of something mundane. The room was brilliantly awash in the turtle's light, like they were all causally sitting in the bottom of a pool. His wife and Other Mackenzie were lying on a sectional couch nearly head to head sharing a vape bag. Other Nate sat in a recliner, legs kicked out, and head back. He held a cigarette with a precarious ash between his fingers, seemingly content to let it burn down to the filter. There was a little girl in the other room, her back to them, busily flipping through the pages of an old photo album. It looked like Cindy Abernathy, but he doubted Scott would ever let this crew around his daughter.

"Mackenzie," Nate said. "What the fuck?" The two women looked up at him and shrugged. "That's it? You're not going to say anything?" He walked over to the turtle, picked it off the floor and flipped the control switch to off. The light in the room didn't change.

There was a moment where the strangeness of this phenomenon didn't register. Other Nate started stirring, fidgeting in his recliner like he was trying to get comfortable. He started talking, but it was hard for Nate to make out what he said. He adjusted Douglas in his arms, feeling him slip a little. He pulled the infant up to his chest. He was now looking at the turtle, registering how it was clearly off, and yet the room still glowed with the brilliant color of its artificial underwater sea scape.

"I've seen light like this before," Other Nate said.

"I saw it off the coast at Galveston," Mackenzie said.

"I saw it off the cost at Galveston, too," Other Mackenzie said.

"I was in the Caribbean with some friends," Other Nate said. "We charted a boat out to this old deserted island that used to be a Civil War fort. We were there to get high and drunk and sleep on the beach and swim a little," Other Nate continued, and as he spoke Nate recognized the story as his own. How he and his friends had done the same thing after college. Part of a month long trip they took.

"We'd just taken the last of the Molly and decided to snorkel. The water was so clear, you could see for a mile. I followed this big sunfish into some pylons left from a dock. I got a little turned around and found myself on the outside of the reef over a deep and empty ocean. I saw this circular blob, like a thicker blue fluid floating underneath me, and I dove for it." Nate remembered all of this, but he never dove. He saw the dark blue blob floating underneath him like a bubble in a lava lamp and got scared. He turned back towards the pylons, and found his way through them and back to his friends. "I don't remember what happened after I touched it. I woke up in a hospital in Bimini, alone with no idea who I was. After a few days of calling around they found my stuff at a hotel in Key West. My driver's license said my name was Nate Butler and I lived in this town." He took a drag from the cigarette he'd been letting burn down. "I didn't remember any of that until just now."

Cindy entered the room holding the photo album open. Douglas was becoming difficult to hold. The baby suddenly became heavier than he could manage. Nate dropped the turtle to the ground and in order to hold his son with both hands.

"These pictures are my future," Cindy said as she displayed old wedding photographs of Mr. and Mrs. Paterson.

"That's creepy," Nate said and then weakly called to Mackenzie as he struggled to hold the baby. The task became impossible. Douglas fell to the floor. All the fear that ever existed in Nate's heart surged through his body. The baby landed safely, but before he could pick him back up, Douglas was crawling away. He'd barely ever rolled over on his own. And now he was up on two feet, clumsily at first, and then surefooted after only a few steps and growing in size as he moved further away. The boy was as big as a preteen by the time he was halfway across the room. Cindy, still holding the open photo album, was growing as well. She started walking toward Douglas, reaching out for what was now a fully grown muscular man. In Douglas's last few steps towards Cindy the weight began falling off him as quickly as it appeared. He even shrunk slightly. Cindy and Douglas stood next to one another as a frail older couple. They took one another's hand and stepped into the full blue light of the room as Mr. and Mrs. Paterson.

Nate tried to move towards his son, but found his body felt locked in place. He glanced toward Mackenzie, still able to move his eyes. She and her counterpart were up off the couch and similarly immobilized. Other Nate was on his feet as well, a thin layer of smoke from his cigarette began outlining his body as if he was incased in a thin fog. He could feel himself start to move under the power of the outside force. With great speed he collided with Other Nate.

◊◊
◊◊

MACKENZIE WENT COLD when she saw Nate and Other Nate smash into one another and disappear. She was so scared that she might have even peed a little. Mackenzie felt the gravity of movement, looked over to Other Mackenzie, who had closed her eyes. Thinking that they were about to be slammed together, Mackenzie closed her eyes too, but she could still see. It was as if she watching her surroundings on a screen in a big dark theater. When the Mackenzie's collided, she felt nothing. There seemed to be nothing left of her other then the vague idea she exited, but that awareness seemed to fade as something else emerged. An awareness of *everything* bloomed. Everything she was and everything that could possibly be in the universe and beyond dawned on her like sun breaking the horizon. She felt Douglas and Nate, her parents, and everyone who ever lived. She felt hydrogen and carbon, nitrogen and oxygen, iron and sulfur; the dust of stars and remnants of the first moments of existence. Just as the very last bit of herself disappeared into the effluvia of the universe, there was light. The perfect blue light of the liquid sphere blinked on in the infinite dark distance. It moved toward her, enveloped her, and blinded her with a painful burst of a billion stars. She found herself running out of the front door of her home watching as her husband futilely tried to breathe life back into their old neighbor's body. The memory of what had just happened disappeared quickly. Mackenzie looked on, feeling helpless and frightened. She felt like she was forgetting something, but couldn't concentrate. She was just somewhere else, she thought, but it was too strange, she was in a panic. She held her hand to her stomach. Mr. Paterson was looking in to her eyes and she felt so connected to him, like she knew him more deeply than their relationship could possibly bear. It seemed like he was calling to her as if she was his mother. There was a warm gush underneath her sun dress.

"He's gone," Nate said.

"Fuck," Mackenzie said. "My water broke."

Beachfront

WE ARRIVE, ONE AT A TIME, at our Grand-Pop's shore house. We claim rooms like it's a free for all. Mom already has one of the master bedrooms and Dad is nowhere to be found. We don't remember the last time we've all been under the same roof. Maybe it was a holiday, we think Christmas, ten years ago. Grand-Pop bought this house after World War II for next to nothing. The house was appraised for two million this year.

Dad, with his hair darker than it was when we were little, is the last one to show. He's with his girlfriend Victoria and their new baby, Star. Victoria holds Star like a barrier between us and her, as if the fact that she is our half-sister might matter to us.

We are not happy to see one another. There are things that we've done that cannot be undone. There is money that won't ever be paid back and words we can't forget. We have stolen our brother's girlfriends and slept with our sister's boyfriends. We have put bloody tampons in our sleeping brother's ears. We've stuck needle holes in our sister's diaphragm. But most of all, more than anything, we were there when our family fell apart. It was the last thing we all did together and it's why our old hurts bloom easily.

In our lives we get by, just barely. We have graduated from being sparring siblings to absentee wives and alcoholic dads. The fact that this is our only chance to own a vacation home is not lost on us. We understand big dreams and little lives.

We watch Dad toss Vic out of the second master bedroom upstairs. It was the room our parents shared, when they were together. Vic gives Dad the finger after he turns his back, then walks into the next open room. Thomas' bags are already there.

"How come you get this room?" Vic asks Thomas. Thomas is lugging in his family's bags from the car.

"I've got the kid and wife, we need the space," Thomas answers and gives him a pat on the belly. Vic has put on a substantial amount of weight since we last saw him.

"We should come up with a fair way to choose rooms."

"Pie eating contest is out," Thomas tells Vic. "You've got an unfair advantage."

"Yeah," Vic replies, rubbing his stomach. "I'm almost as fat as your wife."

The sound of toppled furniture and obscenities draws the rest of us to the room where they're fighting. The pecking order is being reestablished. It only takes a few accidental collisions and some choice words before we're all involved: punching, choking, pulling hair, biting, and scratching. It is strange how our aging bodies remember the violence. We go after each other as if we were in our prime. We don't worry about the toll it will take on our joints and muscles.

"Stop it, stop it! You're acting like children," Victoria says. We all freeze. She is only two years older than Shirley, our oldest, who at the moment has a fist full of Thomas's hair. Even though we are in a ball on the floor she doesn't stand a chance against us.

"She talking to you?" Shirley asks.

"She can't be talking to me," Thomas says.

"Maybe she's talking to me," Lucy adds.

"I can't believe she touches Dad's dick," Vic says. We have her on the verge of tears in seconds. Victoria turns and briskly walks away, which makes us happy. Dad barges in red-faced and huffing. It's like we're all kids again.

"Goddamn it," he yells. "You *will* treat Victoria with respect."

Mom storms in and we think it's just like the old days.

"You ruined my working life Norman," she says with her finger pointing straight at him, inches from Dad's face. "You're not going to ruin my retirement. That goes for you kids too, sort your shit out."

The pecking order has changed. Mom squints at us, gives us her best Malocchio look, and then backs out of the room. She and Grand-Pop were always very close, more like a real father and daughter than in-laws. They used to go fishing for bluefish in the bay all the time. They enjoyed the catching more than the eating. Bluefish tastes terrible. Grand-Pop joked that the perfect bluefish recipe was to grill the fish on a cedar plank, with tomatoes, onions, and lemon. Then toss out the fish and then eat the plank.

When the bags are unpacked and the rooms are divvied up we look around the house. We find Lucy, our youngest out on the deck with Shirley's second husband George. Vic's head is in the fridge putting his hands on our food, opening things, taking bites and then dumping it back on the shelf. Shirley is looking at Lucy and George through a window, scowling at them. She's thinking that this isn't going to happen again. Thomas is helping his wife zip-up a dress that has gotten too small for her. He curses Vic when the zipper breaks.

It is tough to be in this house, just knowing we lurk around each corner. One by one, we sneak out, and then scatter like sand on the dusty windblown beach road Grand-Pop's house sits on. How could we not sell the place? We'll get a good bit of cash in our pockets and then go our separate ways. We are sure most would go for it. Mom will be the toughest sell.

We all start showing up at the old bar. It's funny how we're all hard wired in the head. The bar hasn't changed as far as we remember. It's still owned by the same family that built it in the forties. We sit with our husbands, with our wives, or our young children, but not all together. We find our own spots and order a drink. The plump old lady behind the bar says she remembers us. We used to come in here with Mom and Dad and make a hell of a ruckus when we were kids. This makes us happy and Vic calls out: "Do you remember that B.S. story Grand-Pop used to tell us about the Nazi coming in here for hamburgers?"

"That story is one hundred percent true," The plump old lady says. "I was here washing glasses while my Daddy tended bar."

"No way," Vic says with a smile.

"I swear it," she says. The old lady puts one hand in the air and the other over her heart. We remember the whole story before she tells it. Before the U.S. entered World War II Nazi U-boats trolled the eastern seaboard on reconnaissance missions. One rainy night four German officers landed on Long Beach Island and walked down the street and stopped at this bar. The plump old lady's father served them hamburgers and sent them on their way.

"We weren't at war then," she always ended the story with the same explanation. If her father had known what was really going on he would have taken them apart with his bare hands.

"I don't know if I one hundred percent buy it," Lucy says. We agree with our sister, but it's still a good story, we tell her.

When we get back to the house Mom is in the kitchen holding Star and talking to Victoria. We hear her tell Victoria that Star is a beautiful baby and no matter how bad of a husband Dad had been, he always redeemed himself by making beautiful babies.

"Speaking of beautiful babies," Mom says to Thomas as we file in the kitchen. "How about letting Grandma hold your little boy?"

"Sure Ma," Thomas says and hands little Teddy to her.

"Let's all have a drink together," Dad says. He walks into the kitchen with a bottle of whiskey in his hand. "This was the last bottle Grand-Pop ever drank from."

We raise our glasses to Grand-Pop and cheers him. Then we tilt our glasses to one another and drink. Later, in the night, we sit in a circle on the back porch, wrapped in blankets to fight the chill. Mom and Dad have gone to bed, the kids, the wives, and the husbands are long asleep.

"You know Mom's never going to sell," Lucy says after taking a sip.

"It's been fun," Shirley says. "I'm not going to lie. But, it took a bottle of 90 proof whiskey and I just don't have it in me to drink much that every time we're under one roof."

"Agreed," Thomas burps out.

"You know," Vic says, holding a citronella candle in his hand. "The salt air is very corrosive. Imagine what it's done to the propane tank on the side of the house."

"That'd be a shame," Shirley says, "if something happened."

"Parts of this house are over fifty years old. It might as well be a tinder box." Vic shrugs. "If no one was down here, well, the house could be totally destroyed before a neighbor had the chance to call the fire department."

Lucy holds her drink out in front of her. It stands alone for moment, then one by one, we reach together and clink our glasses. Once all our glasses have touched we knock back the last of the Grand-Pop's whiskey, and then go to bed.

High-Test

THE DRUNKEN PREGNANT GIRL smoking a cigarette in the parking lot of Andy's Airport Inn caught Glenn's eye. She swayed back and forth, dancing without music. Glenn imagined a clear and vibrant melodic rhythm played loud in her head. Despite the bitter cold, her sweat jacket was open in the front, exposing her maternal belly. The leggings underneath her short jean skirt were ripped in a way that seemed purposeful. Her pony tail splashed about behind her in bright blond bursts, made all the more brilliant by the flood light shining down on her. As she danced, she lifted a tallboy in a paper bag off the hood of the car and took a pull. Glenn thought about how easy it should be to feel superior to a person like that, but it wasn't coming easily to him. She danced with the confidence of someone who was impervious to other people's judgment. He envied that. Glenn's cigarette was almost done. Huddled against the bitter cold he lit another and watched her. He made up a little story about the drunk pregnant girl smoking. How she got into trouble, dropped out of high school and moved in with her boyfriend. She got a job at the grocery store, and despite the adversity in her life, she was mostly happy. Her boyfriend, also a dropout, worked at the garage and cheated on her frequently. Her worst fear was being publicly confronted with his infidelity and having to break it off. She depended on him for nearly everything, but was still very proud and unwilling to be viewed as a fool. Even though Glenn's fantasy painted a somewhat underwhelming existence, he envied her for moving out of her parents' house. It was something Glenn had done many years ago. However, due to several setbacks in his life, he was once again living with mom and dad. She stopped swaying, apparently aware she was being observed. She cocked her head and put her hand on her hip.

"What the fuck are you looking at?" she said.

"Nothing," Glenn said. "It's just…"

"Just what, motherfucker?"

"It's just that…" He was drunk and his mouth was dry. "You dance nice."

She let out a delightful laugh. Glenn could tell his comment took her by surprise. He imagined many strangers had offered her choice words regarding the dangers of smoking and drinking during pregnancy. She relaxed her posture and walked over to him. He took a self-conscious drag of his cigarette and nervously searched for other things to focus on. The dumpster, the backdoor of the bar, the full-bright-winter moon.

"I was sure you were going to say something different." She smiled. "You like the way I dance?" Glenn smoked and nodded.

"That's sweet," she said.

"I'm not trying to creep you out," he said. Glenn tried to talk slow and purposefully in order to overcome the slur he perceived in his voice.

"Too late," she said and laughed and put her hand on his shoulder. The creaky backdoor to Andy's was knocked open. A young man with close-cut black hair came out, hands full of packaged goods. He was dressed in white pants, a black belt, and a white t-shirt. Steam came off his bare skin.

"Got the beer, babe," the young man said. He was shorter than Glenn, but muscular with the look of guy who woke up in the morning halfway ready to kick someone in the dick. "Who the fuck is this?"

"This is…" She made the face of a stumped child before she continued. "You know, I don't know who this is."

"Glenn," Glenn said.

"Glenn," the drunk pregnant girl with the cigarette repeated. "He said I danced nice."

"Well, Glenn," the young man said. "That makes you one of the smart ones." He looked directly at the girl. "Is he one of your old regulars from the bar?"

"No," she said. "I'd remember this one. You've never seen me dance before just now, have you?" Glenn shook his head no. "Well, you'll have to come over to *Sugar*

Tops in a few months. Once I get the little one out and start back to work. Then you'll see some real dancing."

"She knows how to shake it," the young man leaned in and gave her a kiss. "Of course if you aren't grossed out by the whole bun in the oven, we could set-up a private show for you tonight." Glenn became aware he'd been nodding along with everything the guy said. "Great," the young man said. "Why don't we head to your place, we'll roll a few joints and Jenny will put on a show. It'll fucking kick ass," the young man leaned to Glenn. "You pay nice and she'll treat you nice." Glenn realized that he was still nodding to the couple and stopped himself.

"It sounds great," he said. "But I can't tonight. Work in the morning, you know how it is."

"Yeah," the young man said. He looked Glenn up and down. He was obviously annoyed. "Let's go babe, this limp dick is all talk."

"Nice to meet you," Glenn put out his hand, but the gesture was ignored. Glenn turned towards the door and started back inside. He had a half of a beer and glass of whiskey waiting for him.

◊◊

THE NEXT MORNING Glenn woke up with his head on the wrong end of the bed. He didn't feel well and wasn't sure how or when he got home. He sat up and pulled the blankets off himself. His chest was bare, but his pants, belt, shoes and socks were still on. He noticed that his lamp was no longer on the night stand next to his bed and found it had been knocked over along with a bunch of pint glasses. He routinely brought them to bed with him, filled with water, in case he woke up thirsty in the middle of the night. Glenn stood up. The rug was soaked, but at least none of the glasses broke. He thought about the noise it must have made and wondered if it had woken his parents.

With an appropriate amount of self-loathing, Glenn made his way to the bathroom. He commenced his ritual and jumped into an ice cold shower. He flushed his nose with a Neti pot, brushed his teeth, took six aspirin, three B vitamins, some zinc, and then downed an energy shot. After all that, he still felt like shit.

❖❖

"BIG NIGHT LAST NIGHT?" Glenn's dad entered the kitchen as Glenn poured himself a bowl of cereal.

"Yeah, you know," Glenn said. "Mondays." His dad nodded.

"You didn't happen to hear some kind of calamity last night, did you?" Glenn asked.

"I didn't," his dad said, which immediately soothed his white hot embarrassment. "But your mother did."

"Awesome," Glenn said and spooned his breakfast into his mouth. "I don't remember what happened."

"Well, your mother sent me to check on you. I asked if you were alright and you said yes." He took a sip of juice. "That's it."

"That's not so bad," Glenn said. "I got into the whiskey last night."

"Ah, the high-test. That'll do it."

"I don't know what's wrong with me," Glenn said without meaning to, an almost involuntary confession.

"Morning, doll-face," Glenn's mother said as she entered the kitchen. She gave him a big smile and pinched his cheek. "So, how are we feeling this morning?" she asked.

Glenn's dad made a hoop by joining the tips of his fingers together and opening up his arms, like a cheerleader making a "P". The gesture was very upsetting to Glenn's mother.

"Aw, honey-bear, what's wrong?" Glenn's mother asked.

❖❖

HIS FATHER'S FAVORITE JOKE was an old clunker about a man who goes to pick up his blind date at a high-rise in Manhattan. The woman is not quite ready to leave so she invites him in. She says she will only be a few minutes. She tells him to make himself a drink and go out on the porch and enjoy the view, which he does. After a few minutes a little dog joins him. While the white fluffy dog is small and harmless looking, it growls at the man and bares its teeth.

"Is your dog friendly?" The man calls into the apartment.

"Yes," she says. "Rollo is very friendly. He just wants you to play with him."

"I feel like he wants to bite me."

"He just wants to play," she insists. "Make a hoop with your arms, he'll jump through them." The man is doubtful, but figures *why not?* He makes a hoop with his arms, the dog stops growling, backs up and gets a running start and then launches itself into the air, through the man's arms and then over the porch railing and off the side of the 15th floor. The man is stunned. The woman appears shortly after and looks around. "Where's Rollo?"

"Rollo seemed depressed," the man says.

❖❖

GLENN ARRIVED LATE TO WORK, which no one noticed because his office was in a satellite building that nobody visited. He shared an office with a woman named Sharon, a fifty something mother of three girls who arrived even later than he did. The first half of his day was made of a series of promises and resolutions that had to do with quitting smoking and drinking less. There was some toiling on the fact that he had moved back in with his parents over a year ago and should be in his own place by now. As the fog of his hangover lifted he attempted to do some work and successfully moved a few items from his inbox to his outbox. In the afternoon he looked through the job posting site at his company and thought about applying for a new job. Something more challenging with better pay. This made him think about the Master's degree in Business

Administration he'd abandoned right before moving back in with his parents, which made him think about his ex-girlfriend, who he'd nearly married, and who was now engaged to someone else. When four fifteen came around, it felt close enough to five for him to leave. *Tonight,* he thought while he drove, *I will just have one and go.*

Glenn decided to go to the bar where his father drank, a strip-mall bar and grill with a lot of flat screens TVs and low light. With family around he would be less likely to go to whiskey and in effect would be cutting back, as he resolved. His father was already there; he was a semi-retired investment banker who made his own hours. The two shared a pitcher. For the first time all day Glenn felt good. The days' worth of discomfort, both physical and mental, washed away. They split another pitcher.

"Well," Glenn's father stood from his bar stool. "That'll do it for me."

"I'll be right behind you," Glenn said. "I'm going to do one and go."

"Okay." Glenn's dad gave him a pat on the back as he left. Glenn ordered another pitcher and drank it while watching the game. His phone vibrated on the sticky wood veneer of the bar. Glenn was excited at the possibility that someone was looking for him. Maybe one of his friends had a night off from his wife and was looking for something to do. Maybe it was his ex-girlfriend calling to tell him she'd made a mistake.

He grabbed the phone. It was a text from his mother. She asked that he go to the supermarket and pick-up a container of Neapolitan ice cream. This was not good. An ice cream order from Mom meant that she was concerned and trying to get him home at a decent hour. The idea being, the supermarket closes at eight and ice cream melts, so without acting like an overbearing mother of a thirty-year-old man (who shouldn't be living at home), she could keep Glenn from staying out all night. However, it was not a flawless plan, not in December, not when it was this cold. Glenn told the bartender he'd be back and left a half drunk pitcher on the bar.

❖

GLENN'S MOM DIDN'T EVEN like Neapolitan ice cream. It would just sit in the freezer until it grew frost and then Glenn's mom would put it out back for the deer to eat. She hated all the deer that made a home in the back of her property and hoped soured Neapolitan ice cream might somehow wipe out the herd. So far the method had been unsuccessful. Glenn grabbed a container of *Turkey Hill* and headed for the check-out lanes. It was fairly empty, being so close to closing. There was an old woman buying a scary amount of cat food so he started for the empty lane a bit further down, but the check-out girl tending to the old woman caught his eye. It was the drunk smoking pregnant girl from Andy's Airport Inn parking lot. He figured that he'd seen her here dozens of times and never took notice of her. Glenn was more excited to see her than he should be. After all, they didn't know each other one bit. However, he couldn't help it, he was thrilled. It was like he'd just run into an old friend.

She gave him a lingering look while ringing up the cat food, but it was clear to him that she couldn't place his face. He gave her a big hello after the cat lady left.

"From Andy's parking lot last night."

"Oh, right," she said. "I was, well. It was late."

"Yeah," he said. "I was really feeling it this morning."

"That's $4.65." She smiled.

He handed her the money and took the change. He felt like there should be something the two could talk about, but it just started to feel awkward. He nodded and mouthed the words *thank you*, picked up his bag and walked toward the door.

"Hey," she said. "I forget your name."

"Glenn," Glenn said.

"Well, Glenn," she added. "Me and Ricky will probably swing by Andy's later tonight. Be sure to say hi, if you're there."

"You can count on it," he said. He fired a finger gun at her and immediately regretted it. Glenn tossed the bag with the container of Neapolitan ice cream in the back of his car and then returned to his pitcher. He ordered one more, watched the rest of the game and then headed for Andy's. Ricky showed up around 11:30 that night. He looked around the bar made eye contact with Glenn and then kept searching. Glenn raised his hand and waved. Ricky gave him a big smile.

"Who you waiting on?" Ricky asked.

"You," Glenn said. "We met last night."

"Right," Ricky said. "Jenny's in the parking lot, come out for a smoke."

❖❖

WHAT WAS HE DOING? Glenn asked himself as he sunk into the soft brown couch in the living room of Ricky and Jenny's condo. He wasn't even exactly sure where he was. Jenny had all his attention on the drive over. They wanted to go back to his place, which he kept saying was impossible. When they pressed him on it, he made up a lie about sleeping on the couch while he finalized his divorce. Still, they seemed pretty dead set on taking the party to him, but once it was clear that Glenn wouldn't give in they offered to take him to their place. Ricky insisted that they stop at 7-Eleven for supplies and asked Glenn to accompany him inside. Jenny waited in the car. He told Glenn to take out a bunch of money from the ATM. He said that they would play money games, and Jenny would put on a show.

"You like how she dances, right?" Ricky asked and Glenn nodded yes. "The more money she gets, the better she dances." Glenn took out three hundred dollars, all he had until next payday. This money was meant to go to his credit card company. Those three hundred dollars were another small step in paying off his debts and getting him out of his parents' house, and back to school. But he was lost in the intensity of their attention and didn't care.

When they got in the car, Ricky insisted that Glenn sit in back with Jenny. They peeled out of the parking lot. Ricky punched the roof of the car and hollered, then Jenny screamed, and Glenn joined in. As the car made a sharp turn Jenny fell into Glenn's lap. She said sorry, but did not go back to her seat. Instead she ran her fingers through his hair and asked him if they were going to have fun tonight. He nodded enthusiastically and she laughed. Her breath was hot and boozy. He could feel her pregnant belly press up against him. She put her hand between his legs and said, "Oh my, you've got a monster." Then she called to Ricky and said, "Glenn's got a monster."

"You lucky dog," Ricky said. He lit a smoke and punched the roof a few more times. "You lucky dog."

◊◊

GLENN SUNK TO THE BOTTOM of the couch. Something was wrong. Glenn didn't have a monster, he knew that. Why were they being so nice to him? Sure there was the money, but this hardly seemed worth the effort. He started to regret emptying his bank account. He decided he would lie about how much money he had, lie by more than half.

The condo wasn't too bad; it was past its prime, but there were a lot of nice things. They had a super huge

3D High Definition television. There was a Blue-ray player and just about every movie you could think of, there were three video game systems, and a laptop sat on just about every free surface. Even though the furniture was nice, nothing seemed to really match, like it was a bunch of people's tastes all thrown together. Regardless, it was all high-end stuff.

"Wanna drink," Ricky asked. He walked past Glenn into the kitchen.

"Yup," Glenn answered. Jenny entered the den. She had on the same outfit as last night, or at least a similar version of it. She turned on the iPod in the sound dock next to the TV and took off her jacket. She had on a skimpy spaghetti string tank top that didn't quite cover her baby belly. Jenny opened a drawer in the entertainment center and pulled out a long fireplace lighter and began lighting candles. She put a cigarette in her mouth, lit it and began to sway, just as she did last night. Glenn felt at ease. Her eyes were closed as she moved around the den. She turned the lights down. It was so effortless and beautiful that it almost seemed like part of a rehearsed routine. The lights were still on in the kitchen and Glenn could see Ricky sharply reflected in the giant television screen. He was clearly crushing pills on the counter with a spoon and then adding the powder into Glenn's drink. Ricky stirred the cocktail with his finger. Jenny moved herself between Glenn's legs and said, "Hey, are we going to have fun tonight?" She ran her hand down the side of his face; he nodded yes. She pulled her shirt up over her full pregnant belly, just below her breasts, the whole time moving hypnotically back and forth. She took the cigarette out of her mouth, blew smoke into the air, and then placed the cigarette in his mouth. She ran her fingers through his hair again and in an act of prestidigitation produced a beautiful crystal glass of whiskey, clinking with ice. "Drink," she said and he did. He would do whatever she asked of him.

◊◊

GLENN WOKE UP ON A BENCH located on the south-bound track of the Ewingville train station. He was so cold that he jumped to his feet and started running for home before he had one clear thought. It took a few moments to come to any conclusion of what had happened. He knew where he was, it was his home town, but he had no clue how he had ended up at the train station. He was four miles from his parents' place, about two miles from Andy's. He checked his pocket and found his keys, no wallet. No jacket for that matter. As the night started to come back to him, he found himself hoping that a substantial SUV would come along so he could throw himself in front of it, but no one was out this early. His car was a block of ice in Andy's parking lot. He cranked the heat and rolled down the driver's side window. Glenn opted to drive home with his head out the window, rather than de-ice the car. He pulled in his parent's driveway, jumped out of the car and ran for the house. He turned around just before entering, went back to the car and grabbed the bag of Neapolitan ice cream for his mother.

Glenn turned the shower on hot and lay down in the tub. He slipped into sleep for a few minutes and woke with a jolt. There was something wrong with him. He didn't feel drunk, exactly; but he wasn't right. He called out of work and got into his bed and stayed there well into the night. The day was filled with fever dreams. He got out of bed, at least once, to be sick. He heard his parents talking downstairs. There were hushed discussions of concern. In the evening, somewhat out of his fog, Glenn sat up in bed and opened his laptop. The first thing he wanted to do was report his credit and debit cards as missing or maybe stolen. He logged on to his bank's site and saw that his credit card had reached its limit. Fifteen thousand dollars, it was almost impressive. The last charge was at 4:30am that morning. They hit a handful of gas stations, a 24 hour pharmacies, and some random all night spots he couldn't identify by name. In just a few hours and in the middle of the night, they had wiped him out. It had taken him a year and half, not paying rent, living with his parents to bring the initial fifteen thousand down to four. Yesterday that was all he still owed. Without those huge monthly payments tying him down he'd be able to go back to school, get an apartment, and get on with his life. Now he had to start all over again, but it felt worse than that. He didn't know what this was. Glenn called the credit card company. They were actually very helpful and said that they would look into the charges. In most cases fraudulent charges weren't the responsibility of the card holder. This put him at ease.

◊◊

TWO WEEKS PASSED before the credit card company reached out to Glenn. In that time, he had all but become a teetotaler. He'd made inquiries with his school about getting back into the graduate program, securing loans, and also found a second job delivering newspapers in the early morning hours. It was good money, and the extra responsibility kept him out of the saloons. Glenn was excited when Karen, the representative from the credit card company, called. He was anxious to get this situation closed and more than ready to put this whole stupid escapade behind him.

"We will not be taking responsibility for these charges," she said.

"What?" Glenn asked. "You said I wouldn't be responsible for fraudulent charges."

"Our investigation concluded that these charges weren't fraudulent," she stated firmly. "We have video of you from the pharmacy. You were clearly at the location. This case is closed."

"Video?" He felt all the panic and dread he'd managed to avoid pour into him. "I want to see it. I was never in those places."

"You clearly were," Karen said. "We are more than happy to share our evidence with you. I'm sending you the video file now. Thank you for choosing Colonial Credit Card Company. This matter is closed."

She hung up, but Glenn remained on the line. He listened to the dial tone as if waiting for a reprieve. The tone went to a busy signal and he hung up. Sitting on his bed, in his parents' house, Glenn opened his laptop and logged into his email. He watched the file Karen sent. It was him, clear as day. He was inside a shopping cart, his arms raised in victory, fists clenched as Ricky and Jenny pushed him up and down the aisles of the CVS. They threw piles of gift cards over his head, filled the cart with water-picks and foot massagers, and mp3 players. A static camera shots showed the register. The cart, with him in it, flew into frame unchaperoned. Ricky or Jenny must have pushed it and let go. It hit the counter and Glenn watched himself slump forward in the basket. The couple walked into frame and Ricky takes a wallet out of the cart and hands the clerk a credit card. Glenn closed his laptop and went down stairs.

"Another quiet evening?" His father asked from the TV room.

"Yes, indeed," Glenn responded. "Another health night." He opened the refrigerator, found nothing of interest, and closed the door. He opened the freezer and spotted the container of Neapolitan ice cream wedged up against a stack of empty ice cube trays. It made him think of Jenny and that night and how all he had to do to get his money back was to call the cops and tell them where she worked. His heart began to beat with a fight or flight flutter.

"I'm going up to the supermarket," Glenn said, half talking to his father, half to himself. Glenn grabbed his keys, got in his car, and turned the engine over. He took a deep breath and drove to the parking lot of the supermarket where he sat for some time. The song on the radio faded to commercials, the DJ talked a bit, and then another song played. His inability to move started to trouble him. Glenn bargained with himself. He got out of the car on the condition that he would stop in the bar next to the supermarket and have a whiskey. It had been so long since he'd had a sip. An agreement was reached.

Glenn finished his whiskey and decided to order a beer. He felt his penance had been paid and since he was about to take the first step in getting his money back, he was entitled to another taste. Once the beer was gone he made his way to the grocery store. He felt calm and his heart beat with a steady and constant rhythm. Once inside, he spotted Jenny. She was on a break, standing next to the gumball machine in the front of the store, texting on her phone. Glenn thought about going straight to her manager, but decided that was cowardly. He wanted to confront her. An old woman stopped to speak with Jenny, and said something that made Jenny smile and hold her belly in her hands. Glenn could see Jenny mouth the words *thank you*. She then took the old woman's hand and placed it on her stomach. Her tummy was much bigger than Glenn remembered. It looked like the kid could pop out at any moment. The old woman laughed, said something, and nodded her head; and that made Jenny laugh and nod too.

Glenn held his phone, ready to call the police, but he didn't move. It felt different, not like in the car. He could make the call, he was sure of it. He could stand the embarrassment and shame of it all, but it didn't feel right. The woman said her goodbyes and walked toward the exit. Jenny leaned on the bubble gum machine and went back to texting. She bobbed her head and tapped her leg to the beat of whatever song she held in her head.

King Bro

LILY FROWNED AND ROLLED her bottom lip after opening my suitcase. She pulled a pair of bunched up cargo pants out and shook them; as if the wrinkles would fly off, like dust from an old dirty rug. She folded them over her arm, then in half, and then laid the shorts over the crumpled mess of hastily packed clothes. She patted the pants with both hands and let out a little noise, as if to say, "There, that's better."

"What did you forget?" she asked.

"Hairbrush, toothpaste, deodorant, and socks."

"Socks?"

"Socks."

"How?" she asked. I shrugged my shoulders.

"Can you come with me?" I asked. "I'll need help with the language."

"Sure," she said. "We'll go after class."

There was a pharmacy on *Calle Princesa*, just a short walk from the school where Lily was studying Spanish. We took the path on the eastern edge of *Parque de la Bombilla* into Madrid. It was late in the day and there were many people lounging on the long grass for *siesta*. The park, although lush and green, had the feel of a desert; there was a dryness that peaked up through the surface and hung in the air. It reminded me of where I grew-up, dusty old Bakersfield, oh how I didn't miss you.

"Mind if we walk with you and your gentleman friend?" The pack of young girls announced their presence behind us.

"Sure girls, no problem." Lily waved them up. "This is my boyfriend Jake. Jake, these are some of the girls from the program. I've told them all about you."

"Nice to meet you." I turned to greet them, four girls in all. It was a blur of short shorts, tight tube tops, bright teeth, and tan skin. "What are your names?"

"Sorry," Lily said. "My fault. This is Karen, Jenny, Lucy, and Tish."

"Nice manners, Lil." Lucy joked. She was wearing these platform flip-flops that must have given her at least three or four extra inches of height. I've never seen such a thing. Once we were past the park and on the *Calle Princesa* the girls were gone—they changed direction like a school of fish.

"What's their deal?" I asked.

"Some of the girls have been getting harassed by the Spanish," Lily told me. "Especially near the park."

"Has anyone given you any trouble?'

"No," she said. "Luckily, I haven't had any run-ins. To be honest, I wonder if some of them have been making it up."

"Why would they do that?"

"I don't know, attention?" Lily pointed across the street. "Pharmacy's there."

The pharmacy was much smaller than I was used to, no aisles to browse, or magazine racks to glance through. It was impossibly white and clinical. There was a tremendous variety of products, all behind the counter, stacked in glass cases from floor to ceiling. I hadn't spoken Spanish since college; five maybe six years ago. Thankfully I had Lily. Spanish was a requirement at her school and she was able to score some quick points by coming on this trip. All told, it would be six weeks of sightseeing and class work for a semester's worth of credit. Initially I had no intention of going with her. She wouldn't be away that long and I didn't really have much European travel money to spare. After Lily and I had a few long talks my plans changed and I eventually booked my plane ticket, eight days in Madrid on a credit card. I was able to rent a room in the dorms for only thirty dollars a day. I had to get my own room because Lily already shared a room with a classmate. The school seemed fine with it. They said I was even allowed to go on some tours with the group.

"Tell her I need a hairbrush," I said. The woman behind the counter looked at me as I spoke, I searched her face for any recognition of the word *hairbrush,* thinking it might be one of those words that just sticks out and you understand, even when it's not a language you know. Like how I know *basura* and *caliente.* "Any *hairbrush* will do," I added. The women continued to look at me blankly.

"Excuse me," Lily said and stepped forward. The woman turned her attention to my girlfriend and I became excited by the thought of hearing Lily speak Spanish. "DO YOU HAVE A HAIR BRUSH," she said, slow and deliberate, the way those ignorant of a language do. "Por him?" She finished by making the hair combing motion and then pointing to me.

The pharmacist got the gist of the exchange and rose from her seat. She walked over to the white metal ladder and slid it to where the brushes were located. Lily turned to me, bright and smiley, happy that she'd gotten the job done. I looked into her eyes and wanted, with all my heart, to say, *you're a fucking idiot.* Not in a mean way, you understand? Like funny. The way I say shit to my friends, just joking around. But I knew, from past instances, that this kind of interaction didn't sit well. Lily and I couldn't kid around like that, which I kind of understood.

We got back to the dorm with time to kill before dinner. Lily wanted to go right to my room because she said her roommate would be sleeping and she didn't want to bother her. I started kissing her as soon as we got into the room, but she was more hesitant than I expected. We'd been apart for a few weeks and I figured she'd be ready to go, but she didn't seem into it.

"Slow down," Lily whispered.

"What's wrong?"

"Nothing," she said. "It's just been awhile. I'm nervous."

"It's okay," I said. I laid her down in the bed and then got the rest of my clothes off. I kissed her again, more forcefully. I wanted her to feel my want for her. I wanted it to be passionate. This shy version of Lily was a real change from what I was used to. I figured everything would be fine once we found our groove. But, she wasn't into it. What was always a wild amusement park ride of fun and adventure felt dull and unenthusiastic. I was only half hard and losing steam, but we pushed through it and I finished and rolled off Lily. I slept for a little while, and when I woke up it was time for dinner.

Lily went down to the common area while I showered and ironed my gear and dressed. The Europeanness of the shower was a problem. They're not built to accommodate the frame of a half Samoan former college football player. I had to bend over and kind of let my ass hang out and wash my head and chest and then turn around to get my rear. There was about an inch and a half of water in the bathroom when I was done. Of course I had left my shoes on the floor next to the sink, they were soaked. Luckily, there was a pair of flip-flops crammed in my bag.

"Hey Jake," Lily said. "Come meet everyone." Lilly waved me over to where she was holding court in the lobby. She pointed to each one of her friends, and said a name. I didn't retain any of the information. It was just Nerd One, Nerd Two, Gay, Chick I'd fuck, Chick I wouldn't. "...and this is Raffa, who I told you about." The first week Lily was here she called every day and each time she called she'd mention Raffa, who was so sweet and helpful, and who she couldn't get along without. I thought Raffa was a chick. When she corrected me I nearly put a hole through my drywall with my fist. I asked if he was gay and she said maybe, but this dude was not gay. He was fat and sloppy and not dressed well enough to be a gay. Although he did have a giant jeweled gold ring on his finger that looked pretty fruity. He stood up and was super short, even for a Spaniard. He put his hand out and said something that sounded to me like *"Banana banana banana"* and I accepted his hand.

"Nice to meet you, Raffa," I said as I squeezed his tiny little fat fingers in my palm. I mashed his ring into his bones and smiled as his eyes welled up with tears. I let him go just as he started to squirm and gave him a slap on the shoulder. "Good to put a face to a name," I added.

"And this is my roommate Amanda," Lily grabbed me by the arm and walked me over to the young girl reading a copy of Don Quixote. "She's just about fluent."

"Well," I said, reaching for Amanda's hand. "Nice to meet you." Amanda looked upset. Her face went sour, and when she took my hand, she squeezed it as hard as she could. She even made a little straining grunt.

"That's everybody for now," Lily got up on her toes and gave me a kiss on the cheek. "Let's eat!"

After dinner we went back to my room and had sex again. After, Lily went back to her room and I slept alone. I woke late and missed breakfast. After wrestling with the shower I ironed some more clothes and put some stuff away. My shoes were still damp from the bathing mishap, so I went with the flip-flops again. I figured I'd retrace the route Lily and I took the other day, around the park to *Calle Princesa* and into the city. Before I crossed the street from the dorms to the park I heard my name and turned. It was Lucy and the girls—they rushed out of the lobby and jogged and bubbled their way over to me.

"Jake, wait," Lucy called out. "Can you walk us through the park?"

"Yeah, sure."

"We're not stalkerotzy or anything," she continued. "It's just that we've been harassed a few times and it's scary."

"Lily said something about that."

"The Spanish men are awful, this one guy called us American whores," Tish chimed in. "But when we're with a guy they usually don't bother us, even if it's Raffa."

Just hearing his name got my blood up. I wanted to grab him and shake him and yell, just like when I flipped out on Dave Nussbaum in the third grade for raiding my lunchbox. I wanted to knock Raffa down and scream, "Keep your goddamn hands off my juice box! It's my juice box!"

"Jake," Karen said. "Could you give me a hand? My shoe strap's come undone." I stopped with her as the other girls kept walking.

"Yeah, no problem." These girls were unbelievable, just attention-demanding machines. If Lilly saw me on one knee fiddling with this girl's strappy shoes while she stood over me in a short skirt, well, dead wouldn't cover it. Another girl screamed and called my name.

"Help," Lucy cried out. "It's a pervert." I told Karen to stay put and jogged ahead. The three girls were huddled together screaming a god awful scream. I rounded the corner and saw him. He was dressed for exercise: sneakers, a loose sleeveless running shirt, and tiny out of fashion shorts. The pervert had his hand up his leg hole. He had his eyes trained on the girls, and was beating it like mad.

"Hey," I called out and the guy froze, hand still on his junk. We stood there for a moment, looking at each other, and then he took off. The cornerback in me switched on, I was after him. It didn't matter how long it had been since I played. That shit was beat into me at one training camp after another. He looked over his shoulder, a clear sign he didn't know his route. We motored across the grass, between the picnickers, and nappers. I had to clench my toes to keep my flip-flops from flying off, which slowed me down. He took a quick right turn onto one of the paths that cut through the more heavily wooded areas of the park and picked up speed.

He wasn't glancing back anymore. He knew where he was going. If he got out of my sight for just a few moments, I was sure he could disappear. His lead on me increased. I thought about Lily and the juice box poacher and it got me mad. I let my flops fall off and was now running barefoot over the rocky pathway. I picked up a few steps on him. There was an opening up ahead, a hub where a bunch of different paths met. I was closing in on him, almost in reach. I felt this burning under my right foot, the same place every time my foot landed. It felt like a pebble was stuck there or maybe I'd been cut by something on the ground. Just as we got to the hub I reached out and got a hand on him. I gave him a push just before he had a chance to change direction. That's all it took to bring him down. He stumbled, then tripped over his own feet, before crashing to the path and skidding to a stop. I was on top of him before he could get back up. I had both of his thumbs firmly squeezed together in my left hand and had his legs pinned down with my knee. The pervert had his eyes closed and was screaming, "Banana banana banana..." over and over. He was a little bloody from the fall, but not too badly hurt.

"Hey," I yelled. His eyes opened and I punched him in the left eye with my right hand. He screamed, "Bananana banana banana..." guttural at first then high pitched and submissive. I felt satisfied by how everything went down. He'd have some swelling and a black eye. He'd have to explain or lie about the marks to his wife, or girlfriend or mother. But I didn't know what to do next. I thought about what I could do to him, what wouldn't be permanent or crippling. When I was a kid

I walked into a plate glass window once and I couldn't see for twenty minutes with all the tears in my eyes. Something like that would give me time to slip away.

"Hey," I yelled again. His eyes opened up and I smashed him in the nose. Blood gushed out immediately and I jumped off him. He just lay there and moaned, holding both hands to his face. I turned back the way I'd come and started jogging. My foot started to hurt more and more. It was cut pretty bad. By the time I found my way out of the park I couldn't put any weight on it. The girls were nowhere to be found.

There was a big fuss made when I got back. The girls had been hysterical and stirred up the whole place. Lily was in tears and looked relieved when I appeared in the doorway. Everybody in the lobby stood up and applauded. I kind of waved and tried to play it as awe-shucks as I could. Inside I was bursting. Lily got under my right arm and helped me to the infirmary. Her roommate was on the phone in the hallway. She hit me with another sour look as we walked toward her.

"Meathead saves the day," Amanda said as we approached.

"Don't listen to her, you did a good thing."

Once we got to the infirmary the nurse gave me some pain pills and bandaged my foot. It started to swell and was at least twice its normal size. I didn't try to put any weight on it. The cut was right across the sole of my foot, from just south of roast beef to my arch. The nurse left me there for the night and then was in early the next day. She examined my foot and seemed pleased. She made a sewing motion and I nodded in agreement. There were a few painful injections and then all I could feel was a tugging on the bottom of my foot. I fell back asleep before she was done. When I woke up my foot was dressed and there were crutches next to my bed. I could still feel the impact and dullness of the pain medication and thought it would be a good time to go visit with Lily. I was sure I'd be in a good amount of pain soon enough. I was pretty good on crutches, another football skill that stayed with me. In no time I was up the stairs and hopping down Lily's hallway.

I heard them as soon as I got on their floor. As I got closer it was clear she and Amanda were fighting. I was thrilled by it, at first. Amanda was such a bitch and I figured Lily was sticking up for me. I stopped at their doorway and listened. I wanted to hear Lily really give it to her. I could hear some of what they were saying, but not enough to understand the conversation. Amanda was insisting Lily do something and Lily wasn't agreeing. I pressed my ear against the door.

"You know you have to," Amanda said, not yelling anymore. "Sooner or later."

"I know," Lily said. And then it was quiet, but not pin drop quiet. I gave them a minute. They weren't talking, but there was movement, the god-awful sound of friction, of intimacy. I banged on the door and heard one of them curse.

"Who is it?" Lily asked.

"It's me, what are you doing in there?"

"Nothing, hold on a second, Amanda is getting changed."

When the door finally opened I felt like I was walking into a crime scene. Amanda was as far away from the door as she could get, standing in the corner holding a magazine in her hand. It was all over Lily's face. She was the guilty type, never able to hide anything.

"What the fuck?" I said.

"What?"

"Don't," I pushed my way past Lily. "What were you doing?"

"Nothing," Lily said.

"What were you doing?" I looked directly at Amanda. She shrugged and tossed the magazine she wasn't reading onto the desk.

"I'm sorry man," Amanda said and put a consoling arm on my shoulder. "I didn't want it to go down this way."

Amanda reached out for Lily as she walked by. She took Lily's hand and guided it to her mouth, looking in Lily's eyes the whole time, and gave the back of her hand a soft full kiss. There was nothing sexy about the touch, nothing hedonistic or wanton. It was caring and affectionate and intimate. Lily brought up her attraction to women a few times before; she'd said, flat out, that she'd bring another girl into bed with us. I always thought it was bullshit, a girlfriend test.

Amanda walked toward the door. She turned and smirked at me before leaving. It wasn't the pure hate

I'd seen from her earlier—I'd swear she felt sorry for me. The door closed and Lily and I stared at each other in silence for a moment. An engine of feelings I didn't understand went into overdrive inside me. I wished for a power to make this all better, to undo and unlearn the things that had just happened in this room. Lily tried to speak and I cut her off.

"I fucked your friends," I said, as stern as I could, but my voice quaked. Lily looked at me, and winced. "Nancy and Samantha and Sandy." These were Lily's oldest and best friends, "I fucked all of them. And not just once either."

"No," Lily said weakly. Her body folded in on itself, like she'd been socked in the gut.

"You can call them and ask them for yourself," I said. "But if they're shitty enough friends to let me fuck them, they'll probably have no problem lying to you. "

"Please," she said with eyes full of hurt. She was on the verge of a full sobbing fit and then just as I expected her to break, nothing. She stood up straight again, and looked me in the eye. It was like whatever thing she held for me, inside of her, had been pummeled beyond the point of repair. "Go," she said and I did.

I had my flight changed and bags packed within an hour. I climbed down to the bar in the lobby and started what I expected to be a good few weeks of being drunk and sad and drunk and angry. No one talked to me at the bar, word traveled fast in this little dorm. Just the day before it was all applause and thanks. One day later, I was an STD sitting on a bar stool. I decided I'd get a cab, after finishing my drink, and spend the rest of the day in the airport. I got on my crutches and made my way up the stairs. Three steps from the top I looked up and saw fat sloppy Raffa standing there, almost face to face with me.

"What the fuck do you want?"

"Banana!" He said and started to swing. He pulled his fist back so far that it took a million years if it took a second to reach my face. I still can't believe he landed that tugboat, but he did. I was fumbling with my crutches and trying to steady myself on one foot while on the stairs. His huge ring landed just south of my eye on my left cheek and it dragged across the bridge of my nose between my eyes, slicing my face the whole way. Somehow I got my hands on the banister and saved myself from falling down the steps and breaking my neck.

There was another day in the infirmary, my face bandaged up like a burn victim. No one came to visit. I slipped out to the airport in the middle of the night and I never saw Lily again. That scar Raffa gave me is still a bright white line across the middle of my face. When I tell the story to friends I leave out the stuff about Lily and Amanda and Raffa. I just tell them about the girls and the pervert in the park.

Some Other Kind of Apocalypse

BLEAKER KNEW the office girls were visiting the site. That's why when he cut the top of his thumb off on the circular saw he grunted instead of screamed. He grunted, guttural like, and made a throaty noise that sounded like he was disagreeing with someone. He didn't go all high-pitched and panicky. He didn't curse or lose his cool or call for his mother or anything that could be considered uncool or lame or childlike or babyish. He just held his hand close to his body, periodically bowed while blood gushed out of his hand.

"The owners are coming by in half-an-hour for a site visit," I said.

"Sorry, boss." Bleaker's bottom lip trembled as he spoke.

"Can somebody drive this dummy to the hospital? Where's his thumb?" I took off my work gloves and threw them to the floor of what would be the Austins' new living room.

The office girls delivered coffee to my work crews once a week and had shown up at the right site, at the wrong time. The girls were huddled together in the framed out front doorway, horrified. I turned off the saw and walked to Bleaker. There were little splatters of blood here and there, and a few big glops pooled on floor clumping piles of sawdust together. Nothing was close to finished in the house, so even if it did stain there were still layers of flooring to install.

"Boss," Bleaker said with a weak voice. I looked at him and retched. He held his injured hand for me to see. The blood ran down his arm like one of those buffet fountain things you could fill with melted cheese or chocolate. His thumb hadn't been all the way loped-off, a little bit of skin and flesh kept it attached. It looked like an open Zippo. The girls screamed and did little heebie-jeebie jumps as if the floor was covered in spiders. Casey was the first to go, she started to puke and covered her mouth, which just pressurized the vomit and made it shoot out like a fire hose all over foyer. Casey caught Tara with the puke spray, and Tara's eyes were already rolling back in her head, so she passed the fuck out, fell right over. I laughed, because holy fuck, right?

I pushed past Bleaker and got down on my knees in the puke and the blood and put my hand underneath Tara's head and propped her up in my lap and kind of rocked her awake. I asked her if she was okay, her eyes fluttered open and she smiled at me as she came to and I got a hard-on, I don't know why. I don't think she knew, but if she did, she just kept smiling. Over all the pungent odors of blood and puke and the smoke of power tools in need of upkeep, I could smell the flower shampoo in Tara's hair. It lit me up, stronger than any energy drink. I asked her if she was okay, she nodded yes. Her smile got bigger and brighter, like I was her hero and something to be amazed by.

"Pip," I yelled. "Help me get Bleaker to the hospital." I looked back to Tara. She was still smiling and looking up at me and blinking her giant Disney Princess eyes. "You alright, sweetie?" She nodded yes. I pushed her brown hair from her face and placed it behind her ear. "You need to head home and get some rest. OK? Take care of yourself." She nodded yes again.

I DIDN'T WANT TO LEAVE my wife and son just because Tara was hot, or that I that I didn't love my wife, or hated being a dad. It was because of the everyday shit. I just couldn't take the everyday anymore. Get up, take the kid to daycare, drive to a site, fight with the crew, work at a site, go to another site, fight with that crew, try to stop at the bar for a drink, get in a fight with my wife, go straight home, eat, watch TV, put the kid to bed, drink, fight with my wife, wake up drunk on the couch at 3AM, go upstairs to bed, try not to wake my wife, wake my wife, fight, sleep. Get up, repeat. No thanks.

I was acknowledged in a grand fashion as I entered the bar. Word about Bleaker and the circular saw was already out in the world. I ordered a beer and told everyone about big dumb Bleaker and his stupid thumb. All the old regulars laughed and laughed and bought me drinks and made their own jokes. It was great, just a real fun, and funny night. The only down side is that my wife kept texting me with the same shit over and over. I told her to come out and meet me at the bar, like she used to do. *Drop the kid off at her parents*, I told her, *come out, have few drinks.* SOCIAL-IZE. But she wouldn't have it. Said the kid was fussy and I needed to come home. I said I would, but stayed anyway. I knew we were going to fight, so I decided to have a few more pops before getting into it.

Tara texted and thanked me for giving her the afternoon off and I texted her back *no problem* and she texted me again and then we were just going back and forth for like an hour. She sent me a pic of her face and her bottom lip was rolled over and pouty. The picture was captioned and said, *I hurt myself.* I asked her how bad and she said *want to see?* And I said *yes-smiley face* and she sent me a pic of the bruise she got from passing out. It was just below her hip and she had to pull her shorts down to show it off. I could see the top of her shorts rolled over in the bottom pic and see how she was holding them down to expose her hip and upper thigh, and a side view of her butt, and there was a tiny blossom of purple from where her panties were rolled over in her shorts. And then she told me that she hurt her ribs too and sent me a pic with her shirt pulled up and the bottom of her bare breast, *the under boob*, clearly on display. The picture showed no bruise anywhere in that area of her body and she wrote captioned the pic and it said *can you make me feel better?*

When I got home, me and the wife got right into it. But it was late, and the kid had already gone down so we did the thing where we whisper yelled at one another and made big hand gestures. I told her I worked hard and needed to socialize, to have fun, and blow off steam. She said she loved to get shitfaced too, but our son, *you know? The KID! Things had changed,* she said, *it was different.* I started to see her side of things and felt like a shitty person, a shitty husband, and a shitty father. We made up a little, started making out, and went to the bedroom. I woke up the next morning with a killer hangover and the *everyday* started again.

"I don't want to be married anymore," I told her.

"I don't know what you're talking about," Maggie said as she picked the baby out of the crib and bopped him around. "I *do* know that daycare starts in an hour and I have to be at work in twenty minutes and our child needs to be washed, fed, and dressed. So I'm going to take care of that, like I always do. Why don't you take some time to yourself and think about what the difference is between what you want to do and what your obligations are?"

After I told her my mind was made-up it felt like an elephant had been lifted off my chest. I kept the news to myself for a bit, I figured Maggie should have time to let it sink in before it became common knowledge. I'd only tell the girls anyway, and they were on vacation.

I skipped the site visits and spent the day in the empty office. We had four remodels and two additions in the work rotation; that was on top of the Austins' rebuild from a total tear down. I reviewed plans, returned emails from irate home owners who thought the work was going too slow, and smoked a bowl. I locked-up, cleaned-up, and went upstairs to the apartment over the office. Usually, we rented the place out, but it had been vacant for about three months. It was a small utilitarian apartment that smelled of mold. It was the kind of apartment you would only move into if you had to. It was your basic last chance before being totally destitute kind of place. Most of our tenants were drunkards who'd lost their driver's license or were working just enough to cover rent and drinks. The last guy who lived there was a *wash* addicted. I remembered after finding the cabinets filled with neatly organized empty bottles of *Scope*. I texted Maggie and let her know that I would be by in the morning to pick the kid up and would leave some money, for bills or whatever, in the kitchen. She replied, *fine,* which seemed overly brief. After setting up the army cot, I left for the bar.

There was no relief that first day out of the house. I woke with a powerful hangover and a poor recollection of how I got back to the apartment. There were no toiletries in the bathroom and the gas to the second floor had been shut off. The water in the shower was freezing. I used the powder soap from the office bathroom as shampoo, and baking soda from the refrigerator to clean my teeth. Maggie was red faced angry when I showed up to the house a few minutes late, she handed me the kid on her way to the car.

"Leave the money in the mailbox," Maggie said and left. It was abrupt and angry, so much so that I felt a little shot of regret right in my gut. I stood, dumbly, on the walkway bouncing my son up and down in my arms. I'd spent all the money last night. I watched Maggie leave and then took my son to day care.

TOM WEXLER WAS at least twice as fat as I remembered him and I swear it'd only been two weeks since I last saw him. He texted me before the noon rush and asked if I wanted to meet him for a beer after work, and I agreed, even though I knew Tom through him being the husband of one of my wife's friends, and knew he had a motive beyond a friendly, no hassle, quality hang. When he asked me where we should meet up I almost told him the salad bar, knowing he never found one in his life.

"What the fuck, man?" Wexler asked as I walked up to the bar.

"Let's take our drinks in the back room," I said and then ordered a pitcher. We were barley three feet from the bar when Wexler repeated himself. "Easy, big guy," I said once we were in the empty game room. "How have you been?"

"Shitty man, real fucking shitty." Wexler took a pull from his beer and made a bitter face. "Can we get some wings back here?"

"What's up?" I said, ignoring his absent minded ask for fired food.

"Don't give me that shit." Wexler leaned in toward me. Sweat erupted from his forehead and ran down the side of his face. It was barely seventy degrees and he smelled he'd been running a marathon. "You left Maggie."

"Well," I said. "It's more complicated than that."

"You sleep next to your wife last night?"

"No."

"It's not complicated," Wexler said. "You're fucking up, which is fine, but your fucking up my shit too." He took another sip of beer and leaned back. "There's a ripple effect, a wake, and I'm rocking in your shit."

"Hey man," I said. "I have nothing to do with your ripple."

"Bullshit," he said. "You're fucking spooking the heard. All the wives are getting jumpy and it's making problems for the husbands."

"That's not my problem."

"Straighten your shit out, or it will be."

"What? Are you and a bunch of other hippos in golf shirts going to beat me up?"

"Fuck you," he said, and relaxed his posture. "Have you done anything you can't take back?"

"What do you mean?"

"You know what I mean."

"No," I said and he nodded at me, got up, and left twenty bucks on the table.

"You won't do any better," he said as he left. I drank the rest of my pitcher and tried not to think about how he was right. Being alone, in the empty Vegas like game room, started my mind going and I didn't like it. I couldn't stand the idea of being in that last chance apartment with nothing to distract me. I stayed and played some songs on the juke box and drank more and thought about the kid and my wife and the office girls and then tried not to think about any of them at all. When I got to the apartment, I had no trouble getting to sleep. I woke up periodically through the night. The wood frame of the cot poked me in the side and the stuffiness of the apartment seemed suffocating, even with the windows open. In the early morning I started to have weird dreams, the kind of dreams that are brought on by discomfort and sickness. I was standing in front of the office and something bad had happened to the town, like a plague or some other kind of apocalypse. Everything just felt bleak and empty. Newspapers and trash blew through past me like tumble weeds. Cars sat in the middle of the street, engines engulfed in flames. A mob of overweight men in golf shirts wearing various types of madras shorts made their way to me. They carried leaf rakes and golf clubs like spears and moved in a close grouping, like the villagers marching on the castle in the old monster movies. Wexler was in the center riding on a pristine red driving mower. He pointed at me and sneered. I woke up covered in my own shit. I stripped in the shower and washed with frozen water, baking soda, powder soap, and a little Ajax I found under the sink. I placed my wet and shitty clothes on the cot and folded it up with all the other evidence of incontinence. Before leaving to pick up the kid, I took the load a dumpster at our closest site, and started the processes of mentally erasing the whole incident from my brain.

BACK AT THE HOUSE, I had the door halfway open with one foot inside before it occurred to me that I should have probably knocked. Maggie was sitting at the kitchen table eating oatmeal and reading something on her phone with a breezy disinterest. She looked over to me and said, "Hey."

"I'm sorry I didn't knock," I said. "I know I should, but I just thought you would be running around."

"It's fine," she said. "Just don't forget to do it from now on."

"Sure," I said. "Here's the money I promised, sorry, I forgot it yesterday."

"No problem," she said and got up from the table and took her bowl over to the sink. "Just put it on the counter. I'll grab Marcus from the crib and will be down in a second." The hand-off was oddly uneventful. None of the scorn or anger of previous pick-ups seemed to emerge. Maggie even told me to have a good day. The split seemed more possible than ever. We'd divide our responsibilities regarding the kid and just kind of tag team whatever came up, maybe even act civil toward one another.

The girls were scheduled to work in the office and I was more than a little excited to break the news to them. They were both turning twenty-one in the next few months and there were going to be all these parties that I could now go to. Casey arrived first, newly bronzed from her beach vacation. She nodded to me as she entered and then sluggishly made her way to the reception desk, dragging her feet on the carpet. She pulled an energy drink out of her purse, cracked it open, and tilted it back until the drink was gone.

"Oh, shit," she said and let out a little burp. "I don't feel good."

"Rough night?" I asked.

"Last night was sick," she said. "We went up to the camp grounds with a bunch of people and stayed up all night."

"Sick," I said. "Listen, I need to tell you something." I was glad that Casey was the first one in, because me and her were like good buddies. We talked and texted a lot, it wasn't like it was with me and Tara. Casey was cool and smart and helped me figure stuff out.

"What's up, boss?"

"I left Maggie," I said. "I'm living in the apartment upstairs."

"Cool, man," she said and drank some of her drink. "Live your truth."

"Is Tara coming in today?" I asked.

"I don't know," Casey said. "She was super turnt last night. We may not ever hear from her again."

"OK," I said. "Well if you hear from her, tell her I need to talk to her."

"Is she getting fired?" Casey asked.

"No," I said. Casey nodded and turned on the desk PC, than got up and fired up the coffee machine. I went upstairs and started cleaning up the apartment. I felt like the moldy smell was making its way to the office, and setting up camp inside my nose. It was just about lunch time when Tare finally showed up. She stumbled in, equally as bronzed as Casey, but more hungover looking. I was sitting at my desk putting together a furniture order of the upstairs apartment.

"Tara," I called out. "I need to speak with you, come on back." She perked up a bit, if only because she seemed startled by being singled out and pulled aside.

"Are you firing me?" Tara asked as soon as I closed the door to my office.

"No," I said. "I just have some news that I needed to tell you. Sit." She took her sunglasses off and perched herself on the edge of one of my client chairs. She blinked, as if she had smoke in her eyes, and smiled coyly, with her mouth tightly closed. It was like there was an implosion of happiness on her face.

"Well, Mr. Bossman," she teased me with her voice. "What's your news?"

"I left Maggie," I said with a giant exhale of breath and excitement. Tara sunk back in the chair. She seemed to let what I said sink in, her happy smile faded, and then turned sour. She folded into herself as if suddenly cold and made herself smaller and further away, just like a little kid did when they'd realized they were in trouble. I reached out to her, my mouth opened, ready to speak, and she started to cry. She shook her head *no*. *No, no, no, no* she seemed to say with every bit of her body. No.

All My Lovers Were Liars, Too

THE WATER HAD A BAD CHOP to it from the wind and the boat fell with a slap over every swelling whitecap. Each time I tried to drink I ended up spilling beer on my shirt or knocking the aluminum can into my front teeth. The Golden Gate Bridge, shrinking behind us, looked like an easily breakable model from a Godzilla movie set. I tried to light a cigarette a few times, but the wind and our speed made it just as impossible as drinking. It was late afternoon, but still bright from the sinking sun above and the reflection shining up from the surface of the bay below. Once we were a little past Alcatraz, Bobby cut the engine. Me, him, and JB lit smokes. Bobby lifted a vial of coke from his pocket and tossed it to JB. The boat rose and sank with the swells. I could feel the drop in the pit of my stomach. JB took a bump and handed it off to me. I hit it and gave it back to Bobby. He used this apparatus he called *the Bullet*. It had a built-in glass straw that filled up with coke when you turned it over. You could take a bump without having to dump the coke out and snort it from another surface. We lit another round of smokes.

I didn't like Bobby all that much, and I'm pretty sure he didn't care for me. He was interested in a girl me and JB knew and was being nice to us because of that. He paid for our drinks when we saw him out, and even bought us dinner once. This boat trip was part of his plan to win us over, or at least to get us to owe him something. Barry Bonds was on his way to smashing the all-time home run record for a season and Bobby offered to take us to the park so we could watch the record-breaking run fly into the bay with our own eyes.

JB sank into the starboard seat. He was staring at me and I tried not to notice. We'd known each other since high school, a decade of friendship at that point. We'd also been roommates for two years by then. It was obvious that something was wrong with him. He didn't look good, like he hadn't been sleeping much. Lately all of our minor exchanges at the house were elusively uncomfortable. Normally I'd ask him what was wrong, but I had been sleeping with his girlfriend on and off for some time. I was afraid he had caught on.

JB introduced me and Martha a few years back and we went out a couple of times. JB and her both went to the same college and they had a bit of history together. For whatever reason Martha and I didn't work out and she started seeing JB. It didn't take more than a few dates before they let it be known that they were boyfriend and girlfriend. I told myself that it didn't bother me, stuff like that had happened between me and him a bunch of times over the years. We dated the same girls on and off in high school. On more than one occasion we stepped over one another to get with this one or that one. But there was something about what happened with Martha that nagged at me. I tried to set aside the feeling as best I could and eventually it was so muted that I didn't think it was an issue. A big part of that was Zelda. Martha introduced me to her. She was another college friend that moved out to San Francisco after graduation. We hit it off pretty good and started dating.

Me and Zelda dated for a while and fell into a real good relationship. It was nice and easy and I wasn't anxious or stressed all the time. In those ways it was better than any relationship I'd ever had before. We had similar interests, drinking, fucking, and watching TV. I messed up our good run before too long. We were day drinking on a Sunday at Joxer Daly's Pub in West Portal. At some point in the day we went back my place to fool around. I was sitting up in the bed and she was lying in my arms looking up at me, I gave her a kiss and said, "You're dying to marry me." I was kidding. I liked to tease her sometimes and she liked it too, but sometimes I'd go too far and upset her. We had never talked about marriage before and I was too dumb to realize how serious she'd take it.

"Yes," she said. "I would love to marry you." Her cheeks went red and she turned her face into my lap to hide her embarrassment. That night, when we fucked, I told her I never wanted to fuck anyone other than her for the rest of my life. She lit up like I'd never seen before. The next morning was awkward. Zelda told me how much fun she had and how happy she was. I told her I had a great time, but had trouble remembering leaving the bar and asked her how we got home.

"You drink too much," she said as she dressed. Zelda was a red head with fair skin. She always looked amazing when she was angry. I shrugged, and then she left.

⋄⋄

THERE WERE SO MANY BOATS in McCovey Cove that we couldn't get anywhere close. It didn't matter. We were high and going to be drunk and it was an exciting place to be. I wasn't even a Giants fan. Bobby eased the boat into the crowd and dropped anchor. He opened the cooler and passed around beers, then tuned in the pre-game show on the radio. JB was still staring me down. He caught himself and changed his demeanor, but it kept getting uncomfortable. In a strange unselfish moment, Bobby asked JB how Martha was.

"Good," he said. "She's home in Chicago for the week."

"Oh, shit, I bet you'll be up to no good," Bobby said. He drank some beer and then turned to me, "And how about Zelda?"

"She's good," I said and shrugged. JB rolled his eyes. "We're talking about getting married."

"To each other?" JB asked.

"Yeah," I told him. JB's posture changed completely. He straightened his back bone and sat up like this was the greatest news he'd ever heard. "I mean we're not engaged, yet. We just talked about it."

"But you want to get married?" JB asked. "To her?"

"I don't know," I said. "I think I do."

"Congrats, man." Bobby gave me a bear hug and lifted me off my feet. The movement of the boat caused him to lose his footing and we fell into JB and I knocked my head into his pretty good. We cursed and then laughed it off. After that, we were pretty happy. We drank and smoked and did some more coke. It was good to hang out with JB like this again. It seemed like we hadn't really enjoyed each other's company for some time. Bobby had kept his ulterior motive to himself as long as the coke and beer would let him and then started talking non-stop about Kelly. Me and JB both knew she wasn't interested in Bobby, but we listened to him talk while we waited for the game to start. We turned up the radio as a hint and got him to quiet down for the first few innings, but the worse the Giants played the less Bobby paid attention to the game and the more he brought up Kelly. Even though the Dodgers were pretty much in control of the game the whole time, it seemed like the Giants had a chance to overtake them, and secure a spot in the playoffs. Bobby swore up and down that he'd get us tickets if they made it. He also made us promise to help him hook up with Kelly.

Bonds knocked out his record-breaking home runs seventy-one and seventy-two, neither ball made it to the water, the Giants lost. It wouldn't have mattered even if he hit them out of the park. It was a night game and none of us were dressed warm enough for the weather on the bay. We left at the bottom of the sixth and didn't hear about what happened until we got back to the docks. Bobby invited me and JB out for more drinks, he said he'd buy. It was a Friday and he wanted to keep hanging out. We didn't even bother to come up with an excuse and just told him no. We took the Muni back to West Portal and opted to stop for a few drinks at Joxer's. We talked shit about Bobby the whole ride back. Ganging up on him always brought the two of us closer together.

◇◇
◇◇

THE FIRST TIME I SAW ZELDA after she stormed out was fine, at first. We met at a bar in North Beach near all the strip clubs and Italian restaurants. We talked and drank and laughed and I thought the marriage thing was forgotten. When we got back to my place, back in bed, it was like we were right back in that moment.

"Are you going to remember this?" she asked me.

"I'm not that drunk."

"How do you know?" she asked. "You could be blacked out, right now."

"I'm not that bad," I said. "Not even close."

"Sometimes when you drink you get this look in your eyes, like you're not even there." She adjusted under the sheets, took her panties off, and threw them onto the sofa chair where she kept her clothes in a pile when she stayed over. She left on the ripped and faded *Nevermind* t-shirt that she'd stolen from me on as a nighty. "You get these shark eyes. It freaks me out."

"Doll's eyes," I said, doing my best imitation of Quint from the movie *Jaws*. She made an unhappy face as I leaned in and kissed her. Once she relaxed, I slid my hand under the covers and in between her legs. I started to finger her. She moaned and moved a little bit, then she found my rhythm and her hips began to move and collided with my hand. I was hard. We fucked and then slept and didn't talk any more about marriage that night. The next morning, she was awake before me, just sitting up in the bed. I opened my eyes.

"Are we getting married or what?" she asked.

❖❖

JB BOUGHT THE FIRST ROUND at Joxer's. We knocked our pints together and cheered each other. It was a bit past eleven at night and the bar was busy. We drank there a lot and over tipped all the time so we never had a problem getting drinks and were treated well. Before the first beer was gone it was apparent that throwing Bobby under the bus had lost its appeal.

"Where's Zelda tonight," JB asked.

"Working," I said. She was a nanny and worked for a wealthy couple that paid well and let her live in the apartment over their detached garage, over in Sunset.

Zelda liked the job, she said the little guy she took care of was great to be around and her bosses were easy to get along with. The only catch was that they loved to go out on Friday and Saturday nights, so we rarely got together before Sunday.

"I should call Martha," he said.

"Tell her I said hi," I said. JB gave me a sour smile and walked outside the bar.

⋄⋄

MARTHA HAD CALLED ME AT WORK. This was the week after Zelda had confronted me about the marriage proposal. She had something she wanted to talk to me about and asked if I could meet her for lunch.

"Don't tell JB," she said before hanging up on me. It was strange, but not that strange. Me and Martha spent a lot of time together, but it was always with JB and Zelda. I figured she was planning something for JB's birthday. We met at an empty restaurant by the bay and had oysters with a mignonette sauce and bottle of white wine that she said was good for the price.

"Is JB cheating on me?" she asked, interrupting something I was saying that didn't really matter much.

"Why would you ask me that?"

"I've got a feeling he's cheating on me," she said. "But I also think I might be acting crazy."

"I know what you mean." I poured the last bit of wine into my glass and thought about how much I didn't want to go back to work. "Sometimes I get the feeling that Zelda has this whole life going on that I know nothing about."

"Well," she said. "Is he?" I shook my head and thought about how a few months back we were out and this girl was talking to me and I was flirting with her and JB jumped in and stole her away from me. I knew I wasn't going to sleep with her, but I liked the attention and he couldn't stand to let me have it. He went back to her place and I went home. In the morning he kicked open my door and threw her soiled thong in my face and laughed. I laughed too, like it was the most awesome thing ever, but it wasn't. I hated it.

"I don't know," I said, nodding my head up and down.

"Don't lie to protect your friend," she said.

"It's not like that," I told her. "Let's get some more wine."

"I'm broke."

"Me too."

"I've got a few bottles at my place" she said. "Left over from the party."

I called my boss from a pay phone and told her that I ate some bad oysters and was having sharp intestinal pains. JB and I had come to the conclusion that saying you had diarrhea was the best way to call out of work. It was so embarrassing that your boss would most likely believe you. At the very least they would be too embarrassed to challenge you. I made sure Martha was out of earshot when I made the call. My boss said fine and hung up on me. Most days I'd feel guilty about ditching out on work, but on that day I was already lost in wine-fueled daydreams of what would happen back at Martha's place.

I started to get nervous as soon as we got on the Muni. We took the M from Embarcadero and switched to the N at Van Ness and got off at Cole. I kept wiping my brow with my sleeve to stop the sweat from beading up on my forehead. We got to her house and I plopped down on the futon while she opened the wine. Martha handed me a giant glass, filled to the brim with some cheap California white, and sat down next to me. We talked and drank for a little while without bringing up JB or Zelda.

"I think JB lies to me about where he is and who he's with," Martha finally said. She sounded sad and broken, not as anxious as she did in the restaurant.

"Zelda lies to me, too," I'd said and then we started kissing.

◇◇
◇◇

I HAD CONVINCED MARTHA to get an abortion. I had imagined it was going to be a long difficult conversation between me and her, but it barely took a minute. I think she just wanted someone else to say it first. I told her that I'd be with her after, to take care of her. She was too afraid that it would be suspicious, both of us being out of town on the same weekend. Zelda and JB would both have to know we were gone at the same time and even if they didn't think we were running away together, they'd have to say something, even if they were joking. She decided to go home to Chicago and have it done. She had close friends that still lived there and they would take care of her after.

"She's not picking up," JB said after returning from outside.

"She's probably just out with friends or whatever."

"I don't know." He took a sip from his pint and shook his head. "She's been acting weird lately."

"Girls are weird."

"No," he said. "Like cagey or something."

"I'm sure it's all in your head."

"You didn't tell her I fucked that girl did you?"

"Which one?"

"Fuck you." He downed the rest of his beer. "Get the next round." He flashed a baggie of coke that he must have swiped from Bobby and then tucked it back into his jeans. "I'm going to load up two smokes. Meet you out front."

When we had coke we'd pack our cigarettes as much as we could. We'd slam the pack against our palms for minutes at a time to hollow out the tip of the cigarette. I didn't bother doing it that day and I guess JB knew that, so he went into the john and stuck the cigarettes into the baggie and sucked the coke into them like a straw. I wasn't outside too long, before he met me and handed me one. I looked at the tip of the cigarette, full of white powder, and nodded my thanks to him. I handed him a road soda that I picked up inside and took a sip of my own. At Joxer's, before they got fined for doing this, they would give you beer in a Styrofoam cup and let you drink it while you smoked out front. There were a couple other people smoking, but we lit up anyway. I smoked the cigarette in a couple big drags and then gulped down half of my road soda. The world had changed for the better.

"Fight," JB said to me. He pointed up the street to two guys throwing wild punches at each other in the street.

"Let's go check it out," I said. We started walking up West Portal towards the Muni tunnel where the street came to a T, that's where the guys were fighting. They were swinging at each other without aim or control. Every punch was a well telegraphed haymaker, which often missed or landed sloppily. The pair was moving all over the place. One would throw a volley of swings, backing the other across the street, and then the other would hold his ground and push the other back and start to retaliate. There was hardly any sound, no Indiana Jones exploding thuds when they connected. Just the shuffling of feet and maybe something that sounded like the slap of meat. As we got closer to the fight we could see a crowd outside of the Philosopher's club, the Italian bar in West Portal. We drank there sometimes, it had a nice long bar, and Golden Tee in the back. The bartender was an ex-marine who fought in Granada. He always had rowdy friends in the Phil-Lo club, drinking, other ex-marines, I guessed.

"Fight must have started in the Phi-Lo club," JB said.

"I don't think we should get any closer," I said. "Those guys are kind of all over the place." The brawl came right at us. I took a few steps back, but JB held his ground. The guy being pushed towards us was bald. His white t-shirt was stretched out around the collar from being pulled on and grabbed at by his opponent with crew-cut black hair. I could hear their grunts and strains as they swatted at each other. Mumbled curses punctuated their deep breaths. The bald man made a stand at the curb and pushed the guy with the crew cut back with both hands and then started his charge. I heard laughter come from the group of onlookers outside the Phi-Lo. I don't know if they were laughing at the fight or me for flinching. I was embarrassed just the same.

The fight made it to the other side of the intersection. By then, the Phi-Lo patrons had had enough. They circled the two brawlers and broke them apart. In short order the fight was over and the group was filing back into their bar. We walked back to Joxer's and stood outside the bar smoking and finishing our drinks. JB looked agitated. The mix of booze, the fight, and all the coke were good gas for the angry fire he had inside him.

"I want to fight," JB said.

"What?" I asked.

"I want to get into a fight." He put out his smoke. "I'm going to go into the bar and start a fight."

"You'll get killed."

"How do you know?"

"Because, I'd get killed if I did that and I could kick your ass."

"Then we should fight," he said.

"Okay," I said. "Let's go home first." I pointed up the street. A police car had arrived. It sat parked, with its lights flashing, on the Phi-Lo side of the intersection.

"I'm going to kick your fat ass." JB walked towards me and knocked his shoulder into mine as he passed. I'd never been in a fight before, scuffles sure, but nothing like what we saw at the Portal. I followed closely behind JB. He turned a few times to mock me. It was like he was an athlete pumping himself up for a big game. I stayed quiet and seethed. I thought about how he threw those panties in my face. I thought about the night after my first date with Martha. I told JB how much I liked her, I told him that I was really going to try and make a go of it with Martha. Then a few weeks later, he was dating her. I thought about other fights I had seen, how angry and disorganized they were.

Once we got back to the house, JB turned to me. He put his fists up. Normally it would have made me laugh, but I was scared. I mimicked him and put my fists up, too. I scrunched down, pulled into myself as much as I could and moved towards him. JB was a good three inches taller than me and that would give him a better reach. I moved toward him slowly. I started having trouble keeping an eye on him. The street light directly behind him created a blind spot that he disappeared into. His face lost all definition in the silhouette and it was difficult to make out the edges of his body. I squinted, hoping that would help my vision, but it did nothing. I raised my hand to block the light and I guess JB took that for a first punch. He started to swing. One of his punches landed. I took it better than I expected. He'd hit me on my skull, the left side above my temple. It seemed he did more damage to his hand than my head because he shook it after he hit me. I threw my first punch. He was just out of reach, it landed softly on his chest. He let out a laugh. He swung and caught me again, this time in the chest. It took a bit of my air.

When he was in the blind spot I could only guess where his head was. I moved left, nervous that the next punch was going to land square on my nose. I found I could see better, I kept moving clockwise until the light was behind me. Finally, I had good eyes on him. I could see him in sharp focus and knew the light was giving him as much trouble as it gave me. He panicked and started swinging wildly. I took a step back. It was that easy to avoid him. I pulled my right fist back, stepped toward him and put all my weight into the punch. I caught him right in the face, just below his eye. He stutter-stepped backwards and then fell towards me with his hands out. He grabbed onto my shirt as he fell. I was wearing this nine-dollar short-sleeve button-down I bought from *Target.* For some reason I found myself supremely concerned by the prospect of it being ripped by JB. I decided to just let myself fall with him, in order to save the shirt. I hit the pavement with JB. Instantly something felt wrong. We were face to face on the pavement. He was completely unconscious. I got to my feet. My left arm was pulled close to my body and my forearm was across my chest, as if I was in a sling. There was a sharp pain in my shoulder. I tried to move it, wiggle it around, but the pain grew more severe. I had no say in how my left arm sat on my body. I felt my shoulder with my right hand, a bone protruded out of the socket.

I started to tell myself to be calm and cool. *Be cool, be cool, be cool, breathe,* I repeated. I needed a doctor. I nudged JB with my foot, just shook him a little. He didn't wake. I rolled him onto his back and saw that his face was bloody. My *be cool* mantra changed to *I'm fucked, I'm fucked, I'm fucked, breathe.* I knelt down to examine him and try to see where the blood was coming from. It didn't appear to be gushing out, although his hair was pretty wet with the stuff. He must have hit his head on the pavement in the fall, but I couldn't tell exactly where the cut was. It wasn't from the punch. That was clear. A little red welt had started to blossom under his eye. I started off towards the staircase that led to our front door, but turned back, realizing I couldn't leave JB unconscious in the street. With just one good arm, it was difficult to move his body. I grabbed him by the wrist and pulled, but my new knowledge of how easily shoulders could be dislocated made me think I could just pop his arm out. I grabbed a bunched-up fistful of his shirt, no better. Finally, I stuck my hand in his pants and grabbed him by the belt and waist band. My panic was growing. I abandoned any attempt to move him gingerly. In a few exhausting heaves I had him over the curb and on the sidewalk. I ran in the house and grabbed a tee shirt that had been left hanging over the back of the couch, and a bag of frozen Brussels sprouts from the freezer and went back out. JB was sitting up when I returned.

"You ok?" I asked. He seemed pretty out of it and smiled when he saw me.

"Do you think my mom is happy?" he asked. I helped him to his feet and held onto him as he got his balance. He grimaced and tentatively touched his head with his hand, and then examined the blood on his fingers. "What the fuck?"

"Let's take another trip to the hospital," I said. We moved slowly down the sidewalk towards Junipero Serra Boulevard. The Muni had stopped running and I figured that road was our best chance of finding a cab.

"Who won?" JB asked while touching his eye with his bloody hand. His walk steadied and the blank expression on his face had given way to a more focused look of discomfort.

"Draw?" I offered. We took a seat on the bus bench next to the empty boulevard and waited. A few cars sped by after a few empty minutes, no cabs. My shoulder pain became sharper and more pronounced. The beer and the drugs and the adrenalin were wearing off. The shame and regret kicked in. JB had the bag of

Brussels sprouts inside the t-shirt and was holding it to his head. He muttered fuck a couple times and spit.

As I watched him tend to his hurts I knew it was over, all of it. Us as friends, his relationship with Martha, and mine with Zelda. It was just a matter of time. When Martha returned from Chicago, things wouldn't just go back to normal. You don't just have an abortion and then never think of it again. Could she look JB in the face every day without turning over the decision time and time again? Would she be able to go a full day without thinking "was it JB's baby or was it Ethan's?" And then what? Break it off with JB, shut me out, and Zelda too? Would she try to shove it down and bury it or would she come clean and let everyone know the truth? Martha was a good person, despite all the shitty things she did. She could still mean something to somebody, but not to JB or me or even Zelda. And that meant that I couldn't mean anything to any of them either.

"A while back, Martha asked me if you cheated on her." I said. He leaned forward on the bench and hung his head.

"I didn't say you didn't."

"I figured as much," he said. I felt my mouth fill with words, like vomit. I was about to tell him everything. I wanted him to know I was sorry for being so selfish and petty. I stopped my confession before it poured out of me.

"I'm a bad friend," I said.

"You're a fucking asshole." He stood up and raised his free hand. A cab came to a stop in front of the bus stop bench and we got in.

❖❖

KELLY COULDN'T FLY, she was in her last trimester. I had to go to JB and Martha's wedding alone. I was running late and JB and Martha were already at the altar exchanging vows. Quietly, I took a seat in the last pew. I searched the crowd to see if I spotted any familiar faces. They were all strangers to me. People started to clap. I looked up and JB and Martha were kissing, married. Everyone stood, I spotted Zelda, a few pews in front of me. She turned with a smile to the man next to her. She touched the small of his back and he leaned over to kiss her on cheek.

To growing applause JB and Martha walked down the central aisle. They looked happy in that dreamy kind of way that you only see in the photographs that come in picture frames. I lifted my hand to them as they passed by, but neither seemed to register my presence. I stepped into the receiving line and waited anxiously amongst the other attendees. They were standing shoulder to shoulder, just outside of the church. JB shook my hand firmly when I greeted him. Martha smiled. She looked genuinely pleased to see me.

"Congratulations," I said and gave him a one-armed hug. "Thanks for inviting me and Kelly, she's real sorry to miss it."

"Congratulations to you, too," JB said. "I can't believe you are going to be a father. That poor kid."

"I know, right?" I said and looked at Martha. "Congratulations to you, my dear." I kissed her on the cheek. There was no sign on her face that she was at all uncomfortable with the three of us being together. I wondered if she ever came clean and told him or if it was just something they silently agreed never to speak of. "Well, I'm very happy for you two. And thanks for having me here. It means a lot to me."

"We need to catch up," JB said. "It's been too long."

"That would be great," I said and turned to step away. JB wouldn't let go of my hand. He pulled me towards him, hugged me again. I patted him on the shoulder and we smiled at each other and it felt like we'd moved on, once again, but better this time. I walked down the front steps of the church, through the crowd, across the street and got into a cab and directed it back to the airport.

Acknowledgements

I'D LIKE TO THANK Alexandra Carides, Nava Renek, and the entire team at New Meridian Arts for giving my stories a home. Much of the work in this collection was produced while attending Fairleigh Dickenson University's MFA program. I owe the faculty a huge debt, particularly Tom Kennedy, Minna Proctor, Rene Steinke, David Grand, Walter Cummins, and Ellen Akins. I am eternally grateful to all of the editors who have published my work over the years. It's always a nice lift to have a story accepted. Thanks to my friends, who let me cherry pick their lives—there are versions of these stories with happy well-adjusted people, but no one seems interested. Thanks to my parents who have always supported me and my writing. Emmy, I love you more than words can properly express, everything is much better now that you're here. To my beautiful wife, thank you for making life worth living. I love you with all my heart and would be dead in a ditch somewhere, but for you.

Credits

THE FOLLOWING STORIES originally appeared in these publications.

"New Suit Day" originally in Monkey Bicycle

"Replay" originally appeared in The Literary Review

"Pinball Way" originally appeared in Bull Magazine

"Beach Front" originally appeared in Necessary Fiction

"High-Test" originally appeared in the Atticus Review

"King Bro" originally appeared in Keyhole Magazine

"Some Other Kind of Apocalypse" originally appeared in Open: Journal of Arts & Letters

"All My Lovers Were Liars, Too" originally appeared in Serving House Journal